P9-BAU-111

SHILOH

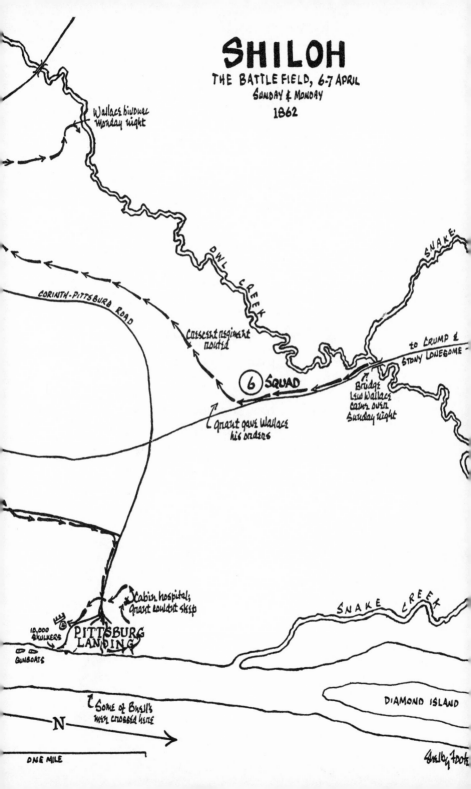

Also by Shelby Foote

TOURNAMENT

FOLLOW ME DOWN

LOVE IN A DRY SEASON

JORDAN COUNTY

THE CIVIL WAR: A NARRATIVE
VOLUME I: FORT SUMTER TO PERRYVILLE
VOLUME II: FREDERICKSBURG TO MERIDIAN
VOLUME III: RED RIVER TO APPOMATTOX

SHILOH

a novel by

SHELBY FOOTE

Random House · New York

Copyright © 1952 by Shelby Foote
All rights reserved under International and Pan-American
Copyright Conventions. Published in the United States by
Random House, Inc., New York, and simultaneously in Canada
by Random House of Canada Limited, Toronto.
First published by The Dial Press, New York.

LIBRARY OF CONGRESS CATALOGING IN PUBLICATION DATA
Foote, Shelby.
Shiloh.
Reprint of the ed. published by Dial Press, New York.
  1.   Shiloh, Battle of, 1862—Fiction.   I.   Title.
  [PZ3.F73918Sh9]   [PS3511.O348]   813'.5'4
ISBN 0-394-40873-X   76-13221

Manufactured in the United States of America
9 8 7 6 5 4 3 2

FOR

WALKER PERCY

CONTENTS

1 *Lieutenant Palmer Metcalfe Aide-de-Camp, Johnston's Staff*

The sky had cleared, the clouds raveled to tatters, and at four oclock the sun broke through, silver on the bright green of grass and leaves and golden on the puddles in the road; all down the column men quickened the step, smiling in the sudden burst of gold and silver weather. They would point at the sky, the shining fields, and call to each other: the sun, the sun! Their uniforms, which had darkened in the rain, began to steam in the April heat, and where formerly they had slogged through the mud, keeping their eyes down on the boots or haversack of the man ahead, now they began to look around and even dance aside with little prancing steps to avoid the wet places. As we rode past at the side of the road, they cheered and called out to us: "You better keep up there! Dont get left behind!" Replacing their hats from cheering the general, they jeered at me especially, since I was the

3

youngest and brought up the rear. "Jog on, sonny. If you lose him youll never find him again!"

This was mainly a brown country, cluttered with dead leaves from the year before, but the oaks had tasseled and the redbud limbs were like flames in the wind. Fruit trees in cabin yards, peach and pear and occasional quince, were sheathed with bloom, white and pink, twinkling against broken fields and random cuts of new grass washed clean by the rain. Winding over and among the red clay hills, the column had strung out front and rear, accordion action causing it to clot in places and move spasmodically in others, as if the road itself had come alive, had been sowed with the dragon teeth of olden time, and was crawling like an enormous snake toward Pittsburg Landing.

Seen that way, topping a rise and looking back and forward, it was impersonal: an army in motion, so many inspissated tons of flesh and bone and blood and equipment: but seen from close, the mass reduced to company size in a short dip between two hills, it was not that way at all. I could see their faces then, and the army became what it really was: forty thousand men—they were young men mostly, lots of them even younger than myself, and I was nineteen just two weeks before—out on their first march in the crazy weather of early April, going from Mississippi into Tennessee where the Union army was camped between two creeks with its back to a river, inviting destruction. This was the third day out, and their faces showed it. Rain and mud, particularly where artillery and wagon trains had churned the road, had made the march a hard one. Their faces were gay now in the sunlight, but when you looked close you saw the sullen lines of strain about the mouths and the lower eyelids etched with fatigue.

We had doubled back down the column all morning, then retraced, and as we approached the crossroads a few hundred yards west of last night's headquarters we saw General Beauregard standing in one of the angles of a rail fence, talking with two of the corps commanders, Generals Bragg and Polk. Beauregard was wagging his head, his big sad bloodhound eyes rimmed with angry red and his hands fluttering. He was obviously upset, which was understandable, for it was ten hours past the time when we should have been pressing them back against the river.

When we rode up they turned and waited for General Johnston to speak, and when he had greeted them with that careful courtesy he always used, Beauregard began to repeat what he had been saying to the others. He favored canceling the movement, returning to Corinth. Just hearing him say it, I suddenly felt tired all over.

"There is no chance for surprise," he said, shaking

his head and shrugging his shoulders with that French way he had. "Theyll be intrenched to the eyes."

General Johnston looked at him for a moment without saying anything, then turned to Bishop Polk (they had roomed together at West Point) and asked what he thought. Men in the passing column turned their heads, watching, but they did not cheer because they could see this was a conference. The bishop said his troops were eager for battle; they had left Corinth on the way to a fight, he said, and if they didnt find one they would be as demoralized as if they had been whipped. He said it in that deep, pulpit voice of his; it was as if I could hear his vestments rustle; it sounded fine. General Bragg said he felt the same way about it—he would as soon be defeated as return without fighting. General Breckinridge, commander of the reserve, rode up while Bragg was speaking. He lifted his eyebrows, surprised that withdrawal was even being considered; he sided with Bragg and Bishop Polk. General Hardee was the only corps commander not present, but there was no doubt which side he would favor: Hardee was always spoiling for a fight.

When General Johnston had heard them out, he drew himself up in the saddle, leather creaking, and said quietly: "Gentlemen, we shall attack at daylight tomorrow." It was as if a weight had been lifted from my shoulders and I could breathe. He told them to form their corps according to the order and to have the troops sleep on their arms in line of battle. As he pulled his horse aside, passing me, he spoke to Colonel Preston.

"I would fight them if they were a million," he said. "They can present no greater front between those two creeks than we can, and the more men they crowd in there, the worse we can make it for them."

I never knew anyone who did not think immediately that General Johnston was the finest-looking man he had ever seen, and everyone who ever knew him loved him. He was a big man, well over six feet tall and close to two hundred pounds in weight, neither fat nor lean; he gave at once an impression of strength and gentleness. His expression was calm as we rode away, but his eyes were shining.

That was as it should be. For this was his hour of vindication after two months of retreat and ugly talk which had followed adulation. When he crossed the desert from California in '61, dodging Apaches and Federal squadrons from cavalry posts along the way, and started north for Richmond from New Orleans, he was hailed as the savior of liberty, and when he reported to President Davis in September he was appointed General Commanding the Western Department of the Army of the Confederate States of America—a long title—responsible for maintaining the integrity of a line which stretched from Virginia to Kansas along the northern frontier of our new nation. That was a lot of line, but no one then, so far as I ever heard, doubted his ability to do whatever was required of him. This was largely because they did not know what forces he had to do it with.

He had twenty thousand poorly organized, poorly equipped troops to defend the area between the mountains of eastern Kentucky and the Mississippi River. By January he had managed to double that number, disposing them this way: Polk on the left at Columbus opposing Grant, Hardee in the center at Bowling Green opposing Sherman, and Zollicoffer on the right at Cumberland Gap opposing Thomas. At each of these points his commanders were outnumbered two and three to one. Hoping to hold off the Federal offensive so that he would have more time to build and shape his army, he announced that his situation was good, that he had plenty of troops, and that he had no fears about holding his ground. His statements were printed in all the papers, North and South. These were high times, everyone still drunk on Manassas and politicians talking about whipping the enemy with cornstalks and the only disagreement among our people back home was whether one Southern volunteer was worth ten Yankee hirelings or a dozen—ten was the figure most frequently quoted, for people's minds ran mostly to round numbers in those days. The general must have known that reverses were coming, and he must have known too that, when they came, the people would not understand.

They came soon enough. First, in mid-January at Fishing Creek, his right caved in: Zollicoffer himself was killed when he rode out front in a white rubber raincoat—he lay in a fence corner, muddy and dead, while Union soldiers pulled hairs from his mustache for souvenirs, and his army was broken and scattered deep into Tennessee, demoralized. Early next month Fort Henry fell to Grant's attack, and ten days later Fort Donelson. Bowling Green was evacuated then, outflanked, and Nashville was left to the enemy, the first real Southern city to be lost. People were outraged. They had been expecting an advance, and now within a month everything had changed; Kentucky and Tennessee were being abandoned without a fight. They yelled for the general's scalp. But when the Tennessee representatives in Richmond went into the President's office to demand that he dismiss the Confederate commander in the West, Mr Davis told them: "If Sidney Johnston is not a general, we had better give up the war, for we have no general," and bowed them out.

That was low ebb, but General Johnston took the blame just as he had taken the praise. He knew that the

9

only way to regain public favor was to give the nation a victory, and he knew that the only way to halt the Federal advance was to concentrate and strike. He chose Corinth, a railroad junction in North Mississippi, near the Tennessee River, as the place to group his armies. Grant, he believed, would try to break the Memphis & Charleston Railroad, which ran through Corinth, whenever Buell reinforced him. General Johnston planned to destroy Grant before Buell came up, after which he would attend to Buell. It was that simple.

So Polk fell back from Columbus, leaving a strong garrison at Island Number 10, and Bragg came up from Pensacola and Ruggles from New Orleans, and Van Dorn was told to march from Arkansas and cross the river near Memphis—he was expected any day. Grant's army was in camp at Pittsburg Landing, on the near bank of the Tennessee River about twenty miles from Corinth. While General Johnston was concentrating, scouts and spies brought him full reports on Grant's strength and dispositions. He knew what he would find at Pittsburg: an army no larger than his own, with its back to the river, unfortified—the only digging they did was for straddle trenches—hemmed in by boggy creeks, disposed for comfort, and scattered the peacetime way. He went on with his plans; he would strike as soon as possible.

By the end of March we were almost ready. The Army of the Mississippi (Beauregard had named it) was divided into four corps: 10,000 under Polk, 16,000 under Bragg, 7000 under Hardee, and 7000 under Breckinridge. We were as strong as Grant and stronger than Buell. Everything was set except for the delay of Van Dorn, who had run into some trouble getting transportation across the river. We waited. On the second of April, Polk sent word that one of the enemy divisions was advancing from the river—heading for Memphis maybe, we thought, though later we found this was not true—and that night a cavalry scout reported that Buell's army was marching hard from Columbia to join Grant. Within two hours of the time the scout reached headquarters General Johnston ordered the advance on Pittsburg Landing. Van Dorn or no Van Dorn, the march would begin Thursday and we would strike Grant at daybreak Saturday, April fifth.

I worked all Wednesday night with Colonel Jordan, assistant adjutant general on Beauregard's staff, preparing the march order. We used the opening section of Napoleon's Waterloo order as a guide—there was always plenty of material about Napoleon wherever Beauregard pitched his tent. First we sent out a warning note for all commanders to have their troops assembled for the march with three days' cooked rations in their haversacks. Then the colonel hunched over the map with a sheaf of notes General Beauregard had written for him to follow. It wasnt much map, really; when I first looked at it, all I saw was a wriggle of lines and a welter of longhand notations, some of them even written upside-down. But as the colonel went on dictating it became simple enough, and after a while it even became clear. I didnt know which I admired the most, Napoleon or Colonel Jordan. I was proud to be working with him.

Two roads ran from Corinth up to Pittsburg. On the map they resembled a strung bow, with the two armies at the top and bottom tips. The southern route, through Monterey, was the string; the northern route, through Mickey's, was the bow. Bragg and Breckinridge were to travel the string, Hardee and Polk the bow. Beyond Mickey's, within charging distance of the Federal outposts, they were to form for battle in successive lines, Hardee across the front with one brigade from Bragg, who was to form the second line five hundred yards in rear. Polk was to march half a mile behind Bragg, supporting him, and Breckinridge was to mass the reserve corps in Polk's rear. The flanks of the army, with the three lead corps extended individually across the entire front, rested on the two creeks which hemmed Grant in. As we advanced, each line would support the line in front and the reserve corps would feed troops from the rear toward those points where resistance was stiffest. That way, the Federal army would be jammed into the northward loop of the creek on the left, or back against the Tennessee itself.

It was the first battle order I had ever seen, and it certainly seemed complicated. But once you understood what it was saying, it was simple enough. I had had a share in composing it, watching it grow from notes and discussion into what it finally became: a simple list of instructions which, if followed, would result in the annihilation of an army that had come with arrogance into our country to destroy us and deny our people their independence: but even though I'd watched it grow line by line, myself supplying the commas and semicolons which made it clearer, when it was complete I could look at it as if it had been done without my help; and it was so good, so beautifully simple, it made me catch my breath. It did occur to me, even then, that all battle orders did this—they would all result in victory if they were followed. But this one seemed so simple, somehow so *right*, that I began to understand how Shakespeare must have felt when he finished *Macbeth*, even if I had only supplied the punctuation. Colonel Jordan was proud of it, too: I believe he really thought it was better than the one by Napoleon he had used as a model, though of course he didnt say so.

It worked so well on paper—the flat, clean paper. On paper, in the colonel's lamp-lit office, when we saw a problem it was easy to fix; all we had to do was direct that corps commanders regulate their columns so as not to delay each other, halting until crossroads were cleared, keeping their files well closed, and so forth. It didnt work out that way on the ground, which was neither flat nor clean—nor, as it turned out, dry. The troops were green. Most of them had never been on a real tactical march before, and many of them received their arms for the first time when they assembled in their camps that Thursday morning; frequently, during halts, I saw sergeants showing recruits how to load their muskets the regulation way. They were in high spirits, advancing on an enemy who for the past three months had been pushing us steadily backward over hundreds of miles of our own country, and they marched with a holiday air, carrying their muskets like hunters, so that the column bristled with gunbarrels glinting at jaunty angles like pins in a cushion.

I stood with General Johnston beside the road and watched them go past, men of all ages and from all sections of the country, wearing homemade uniforms, many of them, and carrying every kind of firearm, from modern Springfields and Enfields, back to smoothbore flintlock muskets which were fired last in the War of 1812. When the 9th Texas swung past, we saw an elderly private who marched with the firm step of the oldtime regular. He was singing.

> "Ive shot at many a Mexican
> And many a Injun too
> But I never thought I'd draw a bead
> On Yankee-Doodle-Do."

The general turned to me with a smile. He too was marching against the flag he had served most of his life. During the period when he was being hailed as the savior of liberty there were page-long biographies of him in all the newspapers, but they were as full of errors as they were of praise. I know because I had the true story from my father, who spent many a night beside a campfire with him down in Texas.

Albert Sidney Johnston had just passed his fifty-ninth birthday at the time of the battle. He was born in Kentucky, the youngest son of a doctor. After two years at Transylvania University he went to West Point. He was nineteen, older than most of the cadets and more serious. Leonidas Polk, the future bishop-general, was his roommate. Jefferson Davis, who also had followed him at Transylvania, was two classes below him. Johnston graduated high in his class and thus was privileged to choose his branch of service. He declined a position as aide to General Scott and chose the infantry. That was characteristic, as youll see— sometimes he behaved like a man in search of death.

While he was a young lieutenant, stationed at Jefferson Barracks, he attended a ball in St Louis where he met the girl he married a year later. She was from Louisville, and I have heard my father say she had the loveliest singing voice he ever heard. In the spring and summer of 1832 she stayed home with her parents while her husband went to fight in the Black Hawk War. When he returned he found her dying. Physicians pronounced her lungs weak, bled her freely and often, and put her on a diet of goat's milk and Iceland moss.

Johnston resigned from the army and came home to nurse her. That was 1833, the year the stars fell. In late summer of the second year she died. After her death he retired to a farm near St Louis where they had intended to live when he left the army. But life was intolerable there, too filled with memories of the things they had planned together. It was at this time that he heard Stephen Austin speak in Louisville and threw in with the Texas revolutionists.

He joined as a private trooper but soon he was appointed adjutant general. When he was made commander of the Texas army and proceeded to his post, he found that Felix Huston, who was serving as acting commander—Old Leather Britches, he was called—felt that being superseded was an affront he couldnt abide with honor. Though he did not blame Johnston personally, he decided his only redress was to challenge him to a duel. He sent Johnston the following note: *I really esteem your character, & know that you must be sensible of the delicacy of my situation. I therefore propose a meeting between us, in as short a period as you can make convenient.*

Johnston replied: *After reciprocating the sentiments of respect and esteem which you have been pleased to express toward me, it only remains to accord you the meeting proposed. I have designated 7 o'clock, a.m., tomorrow*—and signed it: *Your most obedient servant, A. S. Johnston.*

He had the choice of weapons, by the code, but as there were no dueling pistols available and as Huston had no experience with rapiers, with which Johnston himself was an expert, he agreed to use Huston's horse pistols. They were hair-trigger weapons: Huston had a reputation for being able to light matches with them at fifty feet. So Johnston watched Huston's trigger finger and every time Huston was about to line up the sights, Johnston would fire without taking aim, causing Huston's finger to twitch and the shot to go astray. After five wild shots Huston was boiling mad;

17

it had passed beyond a mere question of Honor now —his skill as a marksman was being ridiculed. Years later my father, who was one of the seconds, said it would have been highly comical if it hadnt been deadly serious. Huston finally managed to steady himself, angry as he was, and put the sixth shot into Johnston's hip.

After a slow and painful five weeks spent recovering from the wound, during which time Texas won her independence, Johnston served as Secretary of War in the cabinet. About this time he married a young cousin of his first wife—mainly, my father said, to have someone to mother his children. His share in the Mexican War was limited by politics, but he fought at the Battle of Monterey under Zachary Taylor, whom he much admired. My father was there too and told me afterwards that Johnston fought in the garb of a typical Texan, wearing a red flannel shirt and blue jean pants, a checkered coat and a wide-awake hat; but I was never able to imagine him dressed that way, no matter how hard I tried.

After the war he retired to China Grove plantation in Brazoria County, enjoying life with his family, until in late '49 he was recalled into the U. S. Army by old General Taylor, who had been elected President. Six years later, Jefferson Davis, Secretary of War under Franklin Pierce, gave him command of the newly organized 2d Cavalry, and he spent the next two years fighting Indians on the frontier. Robert E. Lee was his lieutenant colonel, William Hardee and George Thomas his majors. In the late '50s he led his troops against the Mormons out in Utah, and when he returned east in 1860, brevetted brigadier, he was appointed to command on the Pacific Coast, with headquarters at Fort Alcatraz near San Francisco. When Texas seceded he crossed the desert with thirty pro-Southerners and became the ranking field general on the active Confederate list. After him came Lee, Joe Johnston (no kin) and Beauregard.

That was his life, and it was a simple one. He knew disappointments, including the death of the one he loved most in the world, had a conspicuous share in a successful revolution, and knew the humdrum life of a country farmer. Then, at a time when he had every right to think he was through with war and the call of glory, he found himself at storm center of the greatest event of his country's history. At first there had been praise. Then had come vilification. And now, standing beside the road and watching his troops start out on their march against the army that had pushed him back three hundred miles while the clamor of the South rang in his ears, accusing him of incompetence and even treason, there was satisfaction for himself and justification in the eyes of the people.

The weather was clear, not a cloud in the sky when the march began. Regiment by regiment the army lurched into column, rifles dressed at right shoulder shift and the men stepping out smartly, lifting their knees as if on parade. Then the rain began. At first it didnt bother them, not even the abrupt, thunderous showers of Mississippi in April; but soon the wheels of the wagons and the artillery had churned the road into shin-deep mud, and after the first dozen laughs at men who slipped and sprawled, it began to wear thin. There were halts and unaccountable delays, times when they had to trot to keep up, and times—more frequent—when they stood endlessly in the rain, waiting for the man ahead to stumble into motion. The new muskets grew heavy; haversack straps began to cut their shoulders, and there was less laughter and more cursing as the time wore past. Friday, when I approached the column from the rear, the road was littered with discarded equipment, extra boots, sabers and bowie knives, overcoats, Bibles and playing-cards. At one point, four miles out, there was a steel vest thrown into a fence corner, already flecked with rust but gleaming like old silver in the rain.

All that day as I moved along the column I came upon regiments halted beside the road, the troops leaning on their rifles while the commanding general's address was read to them by their colonels. General

Johnston had written it Wednesday night in Corinth while we were composing the battle order.

Soldiers of the Army of the Mississippi:
I have put you in motion to offer battle to the invaders of your country. With the resolution and discipline and valor becoming men fighting, as you are, for all worth living or dying for, you can but march to a decisive victory over the agrarian mercenaries sent to subjugate you and to despoil you of your liberties, your property, and your honor. Remember the precious stake involved; remember the dependence of your mothers, your wives, your sisters, and your children, on the result; remember the fair, broad, abounding land, and the happy homes that would be desolated by your defeat.

The eyes and hopes of eight millions of people rest upon you; you are expected to show yourselves worthy of your lineage, worthy of the women of the South, whose noble devotion in this war has never been exceeded in any time. With such incentives to brave deeds, and with the trust that God is with us, your generals will lead you confidently to the combat—assured of success.

A. S. JOHNSTON, *General commanding.*

I heard it delivered in all styles, ranging from the oratorical, with flourishes, to the matter-of-fact, depending on the colonel. Many of them had been public men, and these made the most of the occasion, adding remarks of their own and pausing between sentences and phrases for the applause of their men, particularly after "women of the South" which was good for a yell every time. But generally speaking the result was the same: the troops cheered politely, lifting their hats, then fell back into ranks to continue the march.

Bragg had almost as many men as the other three commanders put together. Marching all day Friday, he made just six miles, so he had to send word for Hardee to wait for him beyond the crossroads where their columns would converge. It must have galled him to have to send that message, for when I carried a dispatch to him that night at his roadside camp he was hopping mad. He was not yet fifty, a tall gangling man made ferocious-looking by thick bushy eyebrows which grew in a continuous line across the bottom of his forehead. He was a West Pointer, a hero of the Mexican War, and his troops were acknowledged to be the best-drilled in our army.

They got that way because of the strictness of his discipline. I heard once that one of his soldiers attempted to assassinate him not long after the Mexican War by exploding a twelve-pound shell under his cot, and I believe it, for there were men in his corps on the present campaign who would go that far in their hatred of him; or at least they said they would. Anyhow, he left the army about that time and came to Louisiana and became a sugar planter in Terre Bonne parish and I heard he made a good one. I never knew him down there, but I used to hear my father speak of him. Indeed, his name was known everywhere because of what old Rough-and-Ready Taylor was supposed to have said to him at Buena Vista: "A little more grape, Captain Bragg," though later I heard my father tell that what General Taylor really said was "Captain, give 'em hell." When Louisiana went out of the Union he was put in command of her volunteer forces, and later President Davis appointed him brigadier general and sent him to Pensacola to be in charge of Confederate troops down there. He had a reputation for firmness in everything. If his men didnt love him, at least they respected him as a soldier, and I believe Bragg preferred it that way.

Hardee waited, as Bragg had requested, and it was late Saturday evening before all the troops were in position to attack. No wonder Beauregard wanted to go back and start all over again: in his mind, surprise was everything, and he had good cause to believe that the enemy knew we were there. When the rain let up the men began to worry about the dampness of the powder in their rifles; but instead of drawing the charges and reloading, they tested them by snapping the triggers as they marched. All Saturday evening there was an intermittent banging of muskets up and down the column, as rackety as a sizeable picket clash.

And that wasnt all. When the sun came out, their spirits rose; everything that had been pent up in them during three days of marching and waiting in the rain came out with the sun. They began to shoot at birds and rabbits along the road. West of Mickey's, within two miles of the Federal outposts, I watched an entire regiment bang away at a little five-point buck that ran the length of the column down a field adjoining the road. They were Tennessee troops who prided themselves on their marksmanship, but so far as I could tell, not a ball came within ten feet of that buck; he went into the woods at the far end of the field, flaunting his white scut. It was about this time, too, that many of the men began to tune up their yells, screaming like wild Indians just for the fun of it.

And that was not all, either. At one point Saturday evening Beauregard heard a drum rolling, but when he sent orders to have it silenced, the messenger came back and reported that it couldnt be done—the drum was in the Union camp. Beauregard reasoned that if he could hear enemy drumtaps, there was small doubt that the Federals had heard the random firing and whooping in the Confederate column. Our whole advantage lay in surprising them, he believed, and since we plainly had lost all chance for surprise, it was best to call off the attack until another time. That was when he rode away and located Bragg and Bishop Polk, to whom he had been giving his opinion about abandoning the battle plans when General Johnston came up and decided against him. "I'd fight them if they were a million," the general said.

While the troops were deploying for battle, three lines of ten thousand men each, with the reserve of six thousand massed in the rear and cavalry guarding the flanks at the two creeks, the sun set clear and red beyond the tasseling oaks on tomorrow's battlefield. There was a great stillness in the blue dusk, and then the stars came out. The moon, which had risen in the daylight sky, was as thin as a paring, a sickle holding water but unclouded. I never saw the moon so high, so remote—a dead star lighting a live one where forty thousand men, young and old but mostly young, slept on their arms in line of battle, ready for the dawn attack through the woods before them. God knows what dreams came to them or how many lay there sleepless thinking of home.

General Johnston slept in an ambulance wagon. We staff members unrolled our blankets about a small campfire, and for a while we lay there watching the firelight flicker. Every now and then there would be a scrap of talk, mainly about how good it was that the weather had cleared, but it wouldnt last long; presently it would break off of itself, the way talk will do when the speaker has his mind fixed on something that has nothing to do with whatever he is talking about. Finally there was only the deep, regular breathing of the sleepers and the quiet night beyond the low dome of light from the fire and the high dim stars coming clearer as the embers paled.

I thought of my father, who had been a soldier himself and lost an arm in Texas fighting under the same man I would fight under tomorrow, and of my mother who died when I was born and whom I knew only as a Sully portrait over the mantel in my father's study and some trunks of clothes stored in the attic of the house in New Orleans. It seemed strange. It seemed strange that they had met and loved and gone through all that joy and pain, living and dying so that I could lie by a Tennessee campfire under a spangled reach of April sky, thinking of them and the life that had produced me.

Then all at once, as I was falling asleep, I remembered Sherman that Christmas Eve at the academy in Louisiana, the way his tears were bright against his red beard as he walked up and down the room where the headline in the paper told of the secession of South Carolina. I was seventeen then, a long time ago. "You

26

are bound to fail," he said. "In the end youll surely fail."

Now somewhere beyond that rim of firelight, sleeping in his headquarters tent on the wooded plateau between those two creeks, he probably had long since forgotten me and all the other cadets. Certainly he never imagined some of them were sleeping in the woods within a mile of him, ready to break upon his camp before sunup.

Again the sleep came down, but just before it closed all the way, I saw again the vision that had come to me a hundred times before: The battle is raging, flags flapping in the wind and cannon booming, but everything shrinks to one little scene: Sherman in the Yankee brigadier's uniform and myself facing him, holding him prisoner, the pistol level between us. "You see," I say. "You were wrong. You said we would fail but you were wrong," and he says: "Yes: I was wrong. I was wrong, all right," watching the pistol, the tears still bright in his beard.

I had thought I wouldnt sleep. It seemed I ought to make some sort of reckoning, to look back over my life and sit in judgment on what I'd done. But it was not that way. After two days in the saddle and a night in the rain I suppose I was tired enough. Anyway, I went to sleep with nothing on my mind except those few scattered images of my father with his empty sleeve and my mother who was only a portrait (bride of quietness I called her once, remembering the words from Keats, looking up at her looking down out of the frame, immortal like the Greek girl on the urn) and Sherman surrendering to me on tomorrow's battlefield. Before I even had time to tell myself I was losing consciousness, my thought began to take on that smooth bright-flecked whirling image that comes with sleep; I was nowhere, nowhere at all.

There were no drums or bugles to waken us that morning; there was a hand on my shoulder, and at first I could not understand. "Wake up. Wake up." Then I saw Captain O'Hara bending over me and I knew where I was. All the others were stirring already, some standing and buckling their swordbelts, some sitting on their rumpled blankets and pulling on their boots. Last night's fire was gray ashes. That pale light in the tops of the trees meant dawn was making.

We were sitting there, drinking coffee, when General Beauregard rode up. His staff was strung out behind him. Their spurs and sabers jingled pleasantly; their uniforms were sprinkled with drops of dew from the trees. The general looked fresh and rested. He was wearing a flat red cap and it gave him a jaunty air—every maiden's idea of a soldier. As he dismounted, General Johnston stepped out of the ambulance and Beauregard crossed to meet him. They came toward us, accepting cups of coffee from the general's body servant, and when they drew near I was surprised to hear Beauregard again urging a return to Corinth. He was as earnest as before. He said he had heard Federal bands playing marching songs most of the night and at irregular intervals there had been bursts of cheering from the direction of the river. This meant only one thing, he said: Buell had come up, and now there were seventy thousand men in the Union camp, intrenched and expectant, waiting for us to attack.

General Johnston did not say anything. He just stood there listening, looking quite calm and blowing on the coffee in the tin cup to cool it. Beauregard made rapid gestures with his hands and shoulders. Suddenly, catching him in midsentence, there was a rattle of musketry from the right front. It had a curious ripping sound, like tearing canvas. General Johnston looked in that direction, the cup poised with a little plume of steam balanced above it. Everyone looked toward the sound of firing, then back at him.

"The battle has opened, gentlemen," he said. "It is too late to change our dispositions."

Beauregard mounted and rode away, his staff jingling behind him. The rest of us went to our horses. When we had mounted, General Johnston sat for a moment with the reins held loose in his hands, his face quite grave. The sound of firing grew, spreading along the front. Then he twitched the reins, and as his big bay horse began to walk toward the opening battle, he turned in the saddle and spoke to us:

"Tonight we will water our horses in the Tennessee River."

2 *Captain Walter Fountain*
Adjutant, 53d Ohio

I always claimed the adjutant should not even be *on* the O D roster, but when Colonel Appler ruled otherwise and it came my turn I took it in good grace and did as efficient a job as I knew how. When he complained next day about me moping around half dead on my feet, confusing the orders and sending the wrong reports to the wrong headquarters, I would simply tell him it was his own doing for putting me on line officer duty. I didnt require more sleep than the average man, probably, but without at least a minimum I would certainly doze at my desk tomorrow.

Earlier, the night was clear. There was a high thin moon and all the stars were out. However, after the moon went down at half past twelve you couldnt see your hand in front of your face. I had thought that was just an expression, a manner of speaking; but at

33

four oclock, when I made the final rounds with the sergeant, I tried it and it was true. This took careful doing because many of the men had never been on guard before, and after so much picket firing yesterday, they were skittish, ready to shoot at their own shadows. The main thing was not to sneak up on them. I rattled my saber wherever I went and luckily didnt get fired on. When we returned to the guard tent I trimmed the lamp wick, arranged the things on the table, and sat down to write my letter.

On Outpost
Sunday 6 April

Martha dearest

I head this letter Sunday because it is long past midnight. Your poor husband has drawn O D (officer of the day it means) which in turn means he will lose his sleep—But that is alright because it gives him a chance to write to his best girl without the interuptions that always bother us so when I try to write at other times. This will be a nice long letter, the kind your for ever asking for. You know how much I miss you but do not suppose you will mind hearing it again.

The guard tent pen was even worse than usual. While I was scraping it I could hear, above the scree

scree of the knife against the quill, the sound of an
owl whooing somewhere in the trees outside, enough
to give a man the creeps, and in the rear of the tent
the off-duty men were snoring and coughing the way
they always did in this crazy God-forsaken country.

Bango lay with his head outside the circle of light,
eyes shining out of the darkness like big yellow
marbles. He was what they call a Redbone in these
parts, the biggest hound I ever saw. He had been our
regimental mascot ever since a day three weeks ago
we were marching past one of these country shanties
and he came trotting horse-size out of the yard, making straight for the color bearer who was scared half
to death thinking he would lose a leg, at least, but the
dog fell right into column alongside the colors, stepping head-high in time to the cadence. A woman stood
on the shanty steps, calling him to come back, come
back, Sir, but he wouldnt pay her any mind. He'd
rejoined the Union, the men said, and they gave him
a cheer. The color sergeant named him Bango that
same day. Now he lay there looking at me with his
big yellow eyes, just beyond the golden circle of lamplight.

General Grant saw us out on parade two days ago
and held up the entire column while he got down off
his horse to look at Bango. He was always crazy
about animals, even back in the old Georgetown days

when I was a boy and he was driving a logging wagon for his father. He said Bango was the finest hound he'd ever seen.

You would not know old Useless Grant if you saw him now. I keep reminding myself he is the same one that came through home 20 years ago, just out of West Point that time he drilled the militia. He trembled when he gave commands & was so thin & pale, you could see he hated it. Its even harder to connect him with the man that came back from being booted out of the Army for drinking & all the tales we heard about him in St Louis & out in Ill. The men all swear by him because he is a Fighter— & I think we ought to be proud he is from George-town.

It was the operation against Belmont last October in southeast Missouri across the river from Columbus, Kentucky, that first attracted public attention to Grant. He attacked the Confederates and routed them, but his men turned aside to loot the camp instead of pressing the attack, and the Rebels cowering under the riverbank had time to catch their breath. When reinforcements came from the opposite shore, they counterattacked and Grant retreated.

This was no victory. Strictly speaking, it wasnt even a successful campaign. He just went out and came back, losing about as many as he killed. But the fact that struck everyone was that he had marched in dirty weather instead of waiting for fair, had kept his head when things went all against him, and had brought his command back to base with some real fighting experience under its belt.

By then we were pressing them all along the line. When Thomas in the east defeated Zollicoffer, wrecking his army, Grant moved against Middle Tennessee. Gunboats took Fort Henry by bombardment, and when that was done Grant marched twelve miles overland to Fort Donelson and forced its surrender in two days of hard fighting. The Rebels in the fort sent a note asking for terms. Grant wrote back: "No terms except an unconditional and immediate surrender can be expected. I propose to move immediately upon your works."

People back home went crazy with joy, ringing church bells and hugging each other on the street. That was when I joined up. Everybody knew the Donelson message by heart. "I propose to move immediately upon your works"—they said it in every imaginable situation until it got to be a joke. The nation had a new hero: Unconditional Surrender Grant, they called him. Best of all, however, the fall of the forts had flanked the enemy armies. The whole Confederate line caved in, from Kentucky to the

Mississippi River. They fell back, and we followed.

That was when General Halleck was put in command. I saw him once in St Louis; it was in February when I went down after my commission. Old Brains, they called him. He looked a little like an owl and he had a peculiar habit of hugging himself across the chest and scratching his elbows when he was worried. He had plenty to worry him now. Buell moved slowly, careful lest old foxy Johnston turn on him with something out of his bag of tricks, and Grant went off to Nashville (—God knows why, Halleck said; it was clear out of his department) and would not acknowledge any messages sent him. About this time Halleck got an anonymous letter saying Grant had slipped back to his old habits and was off on a bender. So Halleck took Grant's army away from him and gave it to General Smith.

O, my darling it is six weeks today this very Sunday we have been apart. Does it not seem longer? That day that we marched away for Paducah, going to the war & everyone out in their Sunday best to cheer us off, it seems so long ago. In your last you said how proud you were I looked so elegant in uniform, but I was the one should have been proud for you put all the rest of them to shame, & if I was a Captain among the men surely you were a Colonel among the ladies. Such a pretty one too!

*Now you must not be jealous, dearest girl,
because if you could see these country Secesh women
you wouldn't be. They wear mother Hubbards
& are thin as rails every one. It must be because their
men work them so hard I suppose, scrubbing clothes
& boiling soap & everything. They just stand on
their porches & stare at us marching by. O, if looks
could kill. But really I think they would like to have
us on their side——Vain wish!*

When we got to Paducah we were brigaded with
two other Ohio regiments in Sherman's division. That
created excitement among us, for Sherman had been
removed from command of troops in November on
suspicion of insanity. He had told the Secretary of
War that the government would need two hundred
thousand well-trained troops to crush the Rebellion in
the Mississippi Valley alone. But finally Halleck had
decided that he was not crazy, just high-strung and
talkative, and had given him a division under Smith.
Every man assigned to that division was worried.
Naturally no one wanted to go into combat with a
leader who might take a notion to storm a frozen
river or a burning barn. And our first sight of him
wasnt reassuring. He was red-headed, gaunt, skeleton
thin, with a wild expression around his eyes; he had
sunken temples, a fuzzy beard, and a hungry look that
seemed to have been with him always. I never saw

him but I thought of Lazarus. His shoulders twitched; his hands were never still, always fumbling with something, a button or a saber hilt or his whiskers. Our first real operation, however, changed our minds about him—though, truth to tell, it was not a successful movement.

Halleck ordered General Smith to move up the Tennessee River to Savannah—up means south on the Tennessee; thats typical in this country. We went on transports. We were green; most of us had never left home before (officers as well as men, except the officers carried their greenness better) yet here we were, traveling south up an enemy river past slow creeks and bayous and brooding trees. I thought to myself if this was the country the Rebels wanted to take out of the Union, we ought to say thank you, good riddance. The men crowded the rails, watching the swampland slide past. None of them said much. I supposed, like myself, they were thinking of home. It was a strange thing to be in a distant land, among things youd never seen before, all because our people in Congress had squabbled among themselves and failed to get along and there were hotheads in the South who thought more of their Negroes and their pride than they did of their country. Lining the rails of the transports, watching that dismal swampland slide past, there must have been many a man who was thinking of home and the ones he'd left behind.

I miss you So much.

From Savannah, Tennessee, Smith sent Sherman farther south, toward the Mississippi state line, to break the Memphis & Charleston Railroad which passed through Corinth where Beauregard was busy collecting the scattered Rebel armies. This was probably the most important railway in the Confederacy, the main supply line from the Transmississippi to their armies in the East. Two gunboats escorted us up the river. It was good to have them. Everyone, Rebel and Union alike, respected gunboats.

We came off the transports at midnight in the hardest rain I ever saw, and by daybreak we were far inland. Most of the bridges across the creeks had been washed away. The rain came pouring. The cavalry, operating out front, lost men and horses drowned trying to ford the swollen creeks, and behind us the Tennessee was rising fast, threatening to cut us off by flooding the bottom we had marched across. It was agreeable to everyone in the division when Sherman ordered us back to the transports. The gunboats stayed with us going back down the river and covered our disembarkation at Pittsburg Landing, which we had passed coming up from Savannah.

It had been a nightmare operation, floundering in the bottoms. Probably we had done no earthly good. We were wet and tired and hungry and cold. Some of us had been somewhat frightened, to tell the truth. But curiously enough, when we were back aboard the transports where they passed out hot coffee and blankets, everyone felt fine about the whole business. For one thing, we had been into the enemy country— a division on its own, looking for trouble: that gave us a feeling of being veterans—and for another, we had seen our commander leading us.

Sherman was not the same man at all. He was not so nervous. His shoulders didnt twitch the way theyd done in camp. He was calm and ready, confident, and when he saw the thing wasnt possible he did not fret or fume and he didnt hesitate to give it up. Whatever else he might be, he certainly was not crazy. We knew that now, and we were willing to follow wherever he said go.

There is a thing I hope you will do for me, Martha —Bake me one of those three decker cakes like the one you brought out to Camp that day while we were training near home. All I got that time was a single slice. Every officer in the regiment cut himself a hunk & of course Col Appler got the biggest but they all said how good it was. They shall not get a sniff of this one though. Wrap it careful so it wont get squashed & mark it Fragil but do not write on the box it is food because there is no sense in tempting those lazy mail clerks any more than necessary—they are already plump on the soldiers in the field. I can taste it right now it will be so good, so please do not delay.

In peacetime Pittsburg was the Tennessee River landing where steamboats unloaded their cargoes for Corinth, twenty-odd miles to the southwest. There was a high bluff at the river bank—it rose abruptly, its red clay streaked at the base with year-round flood-stage marks. Beyond the bluff, a hundred feet above the water level, there was a rough plateau cut with ravines and gullies. The creeks were swollen now. Oaks and sycamores and all the other trees common to this region were so thickly clustered here that even at midday, by skirting the open fields and small farms scattered there, you could walk from the Landing three miles inland without stepping into sunlight. If you carried an ax, that is. For the ground beneath the limbs and between the tree trunks was thickly overgrown with briers and creepers and a man leaving the old paths would have to hack through most of the way. We spent a rough week clearing our camp sites, but after that was done it was not so bad.

43

The Landing itself was between the mouths of two creeks that emptied into the Tennessee about five miles apart. Looking southwest, with your back to the river, Snake Creek was on your right and Lick Creek on your left. A little more than a mile from the mouth of Snake Creek, another stream (called Owl Creek) branched off obliquely toward the left, so that the farther you went from the Landing the narrower the space between the creeks became. Roughly, the plateau was a parallelogram, varying from five to three miles on a side, cross-hatched with a network of wagon trails running inland from the Landing and footpaths connecting the forty- and fifty-acre farms. It was confusing. When we first arrived, messengers went badly astray going from one camp to another. Guards would roam from their posts without knowing it. All that first week you saw men asking the way to their outfits; theyd gone to the bushes and got turned around and couldnt find their way back. I got lost myself every time I stopped without taking proper bearings. It was embarrassing.

But after we had been there a few days we became used to it and realized what a good, strong position Sherman had chosen. He had an eye for terrain. Those creeks, swollen now past fording, gave us complete protection on the flanks in case the Rebels obliged us by coming up to fight on our own ground. Through the opening to the southwest we had a straight shot for Corinth on a fairly good road (considering) down which we could march when the time came for us to move out for the attack on Beauregard.

Hurlbut's division landed with us. Within a few days the others had arrived, Prentiss and McClernand and W.H.L. Wallace. Lew Wallace had his division at Crump's Landing, downstream on the Tennessee about five miles north of Snake Creek. Our division was out front—the position of honor; they called it that to make us feel good, probably; certainly there was small honor involved—three miles down the Corinth road, on a line stretching roughly east and west of a small Methodist log meeting-house called Shiloh Chapel, near which Sherman had his headquarters. Hurlbut was two miles behind us, within a mile of the Landing. Prentiss took position on our left flank when he came up, and McClernand camped directly in our rear. W.H.L. Wallace was to the right and slightly to the rear of Hurlbut.

There were forty thousand of us. General Smith, who had his headquarters at Savannah, was in command of the army, but it was Sherman who chose Pittsburg Landing as the concentrating point and made the dispositions. We drilled and trained all day every day, march and countermarch until we thought we'd drop, improving the time while waiting for

Buell's army to arrive from Nashville. When he joined, we would be seventy-five thousand. Then the Army of the Tennessee and the Army of the Ohio, combined under Halleck, would march against the Rebels down at Corinth. There wasnt a soldier who did not realize the strategic possibilities of the situation, and everyone was confident of the outcome.

We felt good. When the war began a year ago, all the newspapers carried reprints of speeches by Confederate orators, calling us Northern scum and mercenaries and various other fancy names and boasting that Southern soldiers were better men than we were, ten to one. Then Bull Run came—a disgrace that bit deeper than talk. That was when we began to realize we had a war on our hands, and we buckled down to win it.

Belmont and Fishing Creek and Donelson showed what we could do. We pushed them back through Kentucky and Tennessee, taking city after city and giving them every chance to turn and fight. They never did. If they were worth ten to one of us, they certainly didnt show it. Now we were within an easy march of Mississippi, one of the fire-eater States, first to leave the Union after South Carolina, and still they wouldnt turn and stand and fight.

Of course there is nothing to do but drill drill drill but we did not come down here on a picnic

46

anyway. God forbid—its not my notion of a picnic grounds. Every one feels that the sooner we move against them the better, because when we move we're going to beat them and end this War. Its come a long way since Bull Run—we have taken our time & built a big fine army, the Finest ever was. For the past half year we have beat them where ever they would stop for Battle & I believe this next will wind it up in the West.

Then General Smith skinned his leg on the sharp edge of a rowboat seat, and it became so badly infected he had to be relieved. Halleck put Grant back in command; he had found that the anonymous letter was untrue along with some other scandal about the mishandling of captured goods at Donelson. We cheered when we heard that Grant was back. He kept his headquarters where Smith's had been, at a big brick house in Savannah, nine miles down the Tennessee and on the opposite bank, overlooking the river. We saw him daily, for he came up by steamboat every morning and returned every night. The men liked being in his army. Fighting under Grant meant winning victories.

He was a young general, not yet forty, a little below average height, with lank brown hair and an unkempt beard. His shoulders sloped and this gave him a slouchy look that was emphasized by the private's blouse which he wore with the straps of a major general tacked on. I could remember when he used to haul logs for his father's tanyard back home in Georgetown. There was eight years' difference in our ages: a big span between boys, enough certainly to keep me from knowing him except by sight: but I could remember many things about him. He was called Useless Grant in those days, and people said he would never amount to anything. Mainly he was known for his love of animals. It was strange, he loved them so much he never went hunting, and he refused to work in the tanyard because he couldnt bear the smell of dripping hides. He had a way with horses. Later, at West Point, he rode the horse that set a high-jump record.

When I watched him drill the militia at Georgetown after he finished at the Academy—he graduated far down the list and had almost every demerit possible marked against his name for deportment—I got the idea he hated the army. Seeing him stand so straight and severe, maneuvering the troops about the court-house square, I thought how different this was from what he would prefer to be doing. Then the Mexican War broke out, and though he only had some administrative job down there, we heard that he had distinguished himself under fire, going after ammunition or something.

Next thing we knew, he had married into a slave-owning family down Missouri way—which was something of a joke because Old Man Grant had been one of the original Abolitionists in our county. However much West Point might have changed him, his method of asking his girl to marry him was just like the Ulyss we had known back home. The way I heard it, they were crossing a flooded bridge, the buggy jouncing, and the girl moved over and took his arm and said, "I'm going to cling to you no matter what happens" (she was a Missouri girl, all right) and when they were safe on the other side Grant said to her, "How would you like to cling to me for the rest of your life?"

For five or six years after that we didnt hear of him at all. Then one day everybody knew about him. Stationed on the West Coast, away from his family, he took to brooding and finally drank himself right out of the army. His father-in-law gave him an eighty-acre farm near St Louis. Grant cleared the land himself, then built a log house there and named it Hardscrabble. It was about this time that a man from home went down to the city on business and came back saying he'd seen Grant on the street, wearing his old army fatigue clothes and selling kindling by the bundle, trying to make ends meet. But it was no go. He sold out and went into town, where he tried to be a real-estate salesman.

Now youd think if ever a man had a chance to succeed at anything, it would surely be in real estate in St Louis in the '50s. But that was no go either. So Grant moved up to Galena, Illinois, where his brothers ran a leather business, and went to work selling hides for a living, the occupation he had hated so much twenty years before. Mostly, though, he just sat around the rear of the store, for he was such a poor salesman that the brothers did what they could to keep him away from their customers. He had a high-born wife and four children to support, and at thirty-eight he was a confirmed failure in every sense of the word.

Then came Sumter. But at first not even the declaration of war seemed to offer him an opportunity. He served as drill-master of the Galena volunteers, but when the troops marched away he stayed behind because his position was not official. Then his real chance came. The governor made him a colonel in charge of recruit training at a camp near Springfield, and not long afterwards he picked up a St Louis newspaper and read where he'd been made a brigadier. This had been at the insistence of an Illinois congressman who claimed the appointment for Grant as his share of the political spoils. No one was more surprised than Grant himself.

He was neither pro nor anti on the slavery question,

though his father had been an Abolitionist and his wife had kept her two Negroes with her all through her marriage. A proclamation he issued in Kentucky—"I have nothing to do with opinions. I shall deal only with armed rebellion and its aiders and abettors"— first attracted the attention of the government which was having its troubles with generals who were also politicians. But it was not until the Battle of Belmont that they began to see his fighting qualities. Then the double capture of Forts Henry and Donelson, especially the unconditional surrender note he sent to his old friend Buckner, made his name known everywhere.

This coming great Battle of Corinth will be faught not more than a month from now. The Rebels are massing & we are massing too—& soon we shall go down & get our revenge for Bull Run. After that I'm sure to get a furlough & we shall be together again. It seems so long. Martha, I give you fair warning now—nothing but Unconditional Surrender, I propose to move immediately upon your works. (For goodness sake dont let any body see this not even a peek.)

It gave us confidence just to see Grant ride among us in his rumpled private's blouse, looking calm and composed no matter what came up and always smoking a cigar. (He'd smoked a pipe before. But after Donelson, people sent him so many boxes of cigars he felt obliged to smoke them.) The soldiers never put much stock in all the tales about him drinking and carousing, for we saw him daily in the field. There may have been those little whiskey-lines around his eyes, but they were there before the war. We knew that he had seen to it himself that the whiskey would not get him this time, the way it had done eight years before, and here was how he did it:

He had an officer on his staff named Rawlins, a young hard-faced man in his late twenties, dark complexioned with stiff black hair to match. He'd been a lawyer in Galena, handling legal affairs for the Grant brothers' leather store; that was how Grant met him. As soon as he made brigadier, Grant sent for Rawlins and put him on his staff. Rawlins had a gruff manner with everyone, the general included. Other staff officers said he was insubordinate twenty times a day. That was what Grant wanted: someone to take him in hand if he ever let up. I saw his bold, hard signature often on papers passing over my desk—Jno A Rawlins—and you could tell, just by the way he wrote it, he wouldnt take fooling with. There was a saying in the army: "If you hit Rawlins on the head, youll knock Grant's brains out," but that wasnt true. He was not Grant's brains. He was Grant's conscience, and he was a rough one.

So that was the way it was. There had been flurries of snow at first (the sunny South! we cried) but we were too busy clearing our camp sites to think about marching, anyhow. Soon afterward the weather cleared, half good days, half bad, and Sherman made a practice of sending us down the road toward Corinth on conditioning marches with flankers out and a screen of pickets, just the way it would be when we moved for keeps. It was fine training. Occasionally there would be run-ins with Rebel cavalry, but they would never stand and fight. We'd see them for a moment, gray figures on scampering horses, with maybe a shot or two like hand-claps and a little pearly gob of smoke coming up; then they would vanish. That was part of our training, being shot at.

It was during this period that Colonel Appler and I began to fall out. He had a wild notion that all members of his command, cooks and clerks and orderlies included, should not only be well-versed in the school of the soldier, but also should take part in all the various tactical exercises. That was all right for theory, perhaps, but of course when it came to putting it into practice it didnt work. In the first place they made poor soldiers and in the second place it interfered with their regular duties and in the third place it

53

wasnt fair in the first place. All my clerks complained, and some of them even applied for transfer. One or the other, they said; not both.

So I went to the colonel and put my cards on the table. He was angry and began to bluster, complaining that he could never get his orders carried out without a lot of grousing. He said all headquarters personnel were born lazy—and he looked straight at me as he said it. Finally he began to hint that maybe I didnt like being shot at. Well, truth to tell, I had no more fondness for being shot at than the next man, but I wasnt going to stand there and take that kind of talk, even if he was my regimental commander. I saluted and left. Next morning when I checked the bulletin board I saw that I'd been put on O D for the night.

If this had been an ordinary, personal sort of feud I would have been enjoying my revenge already. Colonel Appler had been making a fool of himself, the laughingstock of the whole army, for the past three days. He was a highstrung sort of person anyhow, jumpy, given to imagining the whole Rebel army was right outside his tent-flap. Friday afternoon, April fourth, a regiment on our left lost a picket guard of seven men and an officer, gobbled up by the grayback cavalry, and when the colonel advanced a company to develop the situation they ran into scattered firing, nothing serious, and came back without recovering the men.

All day Saturday Colonel Appler was on tenterhooks. We felt really ashamed for him. Other outfits began to call us the Long Roll regiment because we had sounded the alarm so often. The last straw came that afternoon. A scouting party ran into the usual Rebel horsemen and the colonel sent me back with a message to General Sherman that a large force of the enemy was moving upon us. I was angry anyhow because I had found just that morning that he'd put me on O D that night, and then after dinner he'd made me accompany him on the scout so I wouldnt have time to get properly ready for guard mount. Now he was adding the crowning indignity by making me carry one of his wild alarms, crying Wolf again for the God-knows-whatth time, back to the general himself. I knew the reception I'd get at division headquarters, especially if Sherman turned that redheaded temper on me. My hope was that he would be away on inspection or something. Then all I would have to put up with would be the jeers of the adjutant and the clerks.

As luck would have it, I met the general riding down the road toward our position, accompanied by an aide and an orderly. When I told him what Colonel Appler had said, he clamped his mouth in a line. I could see he was angry—he'd received that message from the colonel too many times already. But he didnt say anything to me; he clapped the spurs to his horse, and soon we came to a clearing where Colonel Appler and some of his staff were standing beside the road with their horses' reins in their hands.

Colonel Appler began to tell Sherman how many Rebs there were in the woods out front. He was excited; he flung his arms around and stretched his eyes. Sherman sat there patiently, hearing him through and looking into the empty woods. When the colonel had finished, Sherman looked down at him for almost a full minute, saying nothing. Then he jerked the reins, turning his horse toward camp. As he turned he spoke to Colonel Appler directly.

"Take your damned regiment back to Ohio," he said, snapping the words. "Beauregard is not such a fool as to leave his base of operations and attack us in ours. There is no enemy nearer than Corinth."

And he rode away. It was certainly a rebuke to Colonel Appler, administered in the presence of his men. I heard at least one of them snigger.

Charley Gregg has been promoted 1st Lieut in Co G. He bought himself an armored vest in Saint Louis & clanks when he walks. The man who sold it to him said if it did not stop bullets, bring it

back & he would give him another. Ha Ha! You
would not catch me wearing a thing like that—it
would be like admitting in public you were afraid.
The men make jokes about getting him out with
tin snips but Charley likes it & wears it all the time
clanking.

Dawn had come while I was writing my letter. It was cool and clear, the Lord's day and a fine one. Somewhere out front, over toward the right, the pickets already were stirring. There was a rattle of firing from that direction—two groups of soldiers, grayback horsemen and a bunch of our boys, earning a living—but that meant nothing more than that there were some nervous pickets on the line for the first time, itching to burn a little powder and throw a little lead the way they always did, shooting at shadows for the sake of something to write home about. It died away and the birds began to sing.

The guard tent, facing northwest so that the sun came up in the rear, was out in an open field a few hundred yards short of a swale which crossed the center of the clearing. In the swale there was a small stream with a thin screen of willows and water oaks along its banks. The willows were green already but the oaks had just begun to bud. I could see through the fringe of trees the field continuing for a few more hundred yards to where it ended abruptly against a line of heavy woods at its far margin. Sherman's headquarters tent had been pitched directly in rear of the guard tent, out of sight across the road. Shiloh Chapel was to the right rear, visible through the trees which were tinted blood-red now, the color moving down as the sun rose higher.

Near at hand but out of sight, between the guard tent and division headquarters, the cooks were up. I could hear two of them talking above the rattle of pots and pans. I could even recognize their voices. One was Lou Treadway; he was from Georgetown. Back home he always had his pockets full of tracts and was ever ready to talk salvation to anyone who would listen—or to anyone who wouldnt, for that matter. He knew his Bible, cover to cover, and at the drop of a hat he'd expound on a text, usually an obscure one that gave him plenty of room to move around in. He was a little wrong in the head, but a good cook.

"Take that chapel yonder," he was saying. "It's called Shiloh. You know what that means, brother?"

"Cant say I do," the other cook said. By the sound of his voice, he was plenty weary of Lou's eternal preaching. But this was Sunday and Lou was all wound up. There was no way of stopping him.

"Second Samuel, brother"—I could the same as see

him nod his head that positive way he had. "Says it's what the children of Israel, God's chosen, was working toward. Yes: a place for them to lay down their worries. Bible scholars interpret that it means the Place of Peace." And he went on expounding.

Now mind you Martha, no more reproaching me for not writing long letters that give all the news about myself. Here are three pages of big sheets close written—you can not say again your husband never writes you long letters. Guard duty would not be so bad if every man could spend it this way writing to the one he misses most.

Its a beautiful Sunday morn, the sun just coming up. I bet you are sleep in bed. Remember what I said that last night about next time? All the birds are singing.

Birds were tearing their throats out, hopping around in the budding limbs, and there was a great scampering of animals out front in the thickets. It was fine to be up at that time of the morning, even if it had meant staying up on guard all the night before. I didnt feel a bit sleepy, but I knew it would come down on me that afternoon. For the first time, this Southern country took on real beauty, or else I was a little drunk from lack of sleep. I forgot about Colonel Appler and the way he was forever ranting because I misspelled a few words in the regimental orders. The countryside looked so good that it reminded me of spring back home in Ohio, when everything is opening and the air is soft with the touch of summer and fragrant with rising sap and bursting buds.

O my dearest, if only you knew how much I lo

There was a rattle of sound all across the front of the position, like snapping limbs, and another racket mixed in too, like screaming women. Bango lifted his head, the big yellow eyes still glazed with sleep. I recognized it as the sound of firing, and then there were the thudding booms of cannon. Beyond the swale and through the screen of trees along the stream I saw rabbits and fluttering birds and even a doe with her spotted-backed fawn. She ran with nervous mincing steps, stopping frequently to turn her head back in the direction she had come from.

Then I saw the skirmishers come through. They looked tall and lean, even across that distance. Beneath their wide-brimmed hats their faces were sharp, and their gray and butternut trousers were wet to the thighs with dew. They carried their rifles slantwise across their bodies, like quail hunters.

3 *Private Luther Dade*
Rifleman, 6th Mississippi

When I went to sleep the stars were out and there was even a moon, thin like a sickle and clear against the night, but when I woke up there was only the blackness and the wind sighing high in the treetops. That was what roused me I believe, because for a minute I disremembered where I was. I thought I was back home, woke up early and laying in bed waiting for pa to come with the lantern to turn me out to milk (that was the best thing about the army: no cows) and ma was in the kitchen humming a hymn while she shook up the stove. But then I realized part of the sound was the breathing and snoring of the men all around me, with maybe a whimper or a moan every now and again when the bad dreams came, and I remembered. We had laid down to sleep in what they call Line of Battle and now the night was nearly over. And when I remembered I wished I'd stayed asleep:

63

because that was the worst part, to lie there alone, feeling lonely, and no one to tell you he was feeling the same.

But it was warm under the blanket and my clothes had dried and I could feel my new rifle through the cloth where I had laid it to be safe from the dew when I wrapped the covers round me. Then it was the same as if theyd all gone away, or *I* had; I was back home with my brothers and sisters again, myself the oldest by over a year, and they were gathered around to tell me goodbye the way they did a month ago when I left to join up in Corinth after General Beauregard sent word that all true men were needed to save the country. That was the way he said it. I was just going to tell them I would be back with a Yankee sword for the fireplace, like pa did with the Mexican one, when I heard somebody talking in a hard clear voice not like any of *my* folks, and when I looked up it was Sergeant Tyree.

"Roll out there," he said. "Roll out to fight."

I had gone to sleep and dreamed of home, but here I was, away up in Tennessee, further from Ithaca and Jordan County than I'd ever been in all my life before. It was Sunday already and we were fixing to hit them where they had their backs to the river, the way it was explained while we were

64

waiting for our marching orders three days ago. I sat up.

From then on everything moved fast with a sort of mixed-up jerkiness, like Punch and Judy. Every face had a kind of d r a w n look, the way it would be if a man was picking up on something heavy. Late ones like myself were pulling on their shoes or rolling their blankets. Others were already fixed. They squatted with their rifles across their thighs, sitting there in the darkness munching biscuits, those that had saved any, and not doing much talking. They nodded their heads with quick flicky motions, like birds, and nursed their rifles, keeping them out of the dirt. I had gotten to know them all in a month and a few of them were even from the same end of the county I was, but now it was like I was seeing them for the first time, different. All the put-on had gone out of their faces—they were left with what God gave them at the beginning.

We lined up. And while Sergeant Tyree passed among us, checking us one by one to make sure everything was where it was supposed to be, dawn begun to come through, faint and high. While we were answering roll-call the sun rose big and red through the trees and all up and down the company front they begun to get excited and jabber at one another: "The sun of oyster itch," whatever that meant. I was glad to see the sun again, no matter what they called it.

One minute we were standing there, shifting from leg to leg, not saying much and more or less avoiding each other's eyes: then we were going forward. It happened that sudden. There was no bugle or drum or anything like that. The men on our right started moving and we moved too, lurching forward through the underbrush and trying to keep the line straight the way we had been warned to do, but we couldnt. Captain Plummer was cussing. "Dwess it up," he kept saying, cussing a blue streak; "Dwess it up, dod dam it, dwess it up," all the way through the woods. So after a while, when the trees thinned, we stopped to straighten the line.

There was someone on a tall claybank horse out front, a fine-looking man in a new uniform with chicken guts on the sleeves all the way to his elbows, spruce and spang as a gamecock. He had on a stiff red cap, round and flat on top like a sawed-off dice box, and he was making a speech. "Soldiers of the South!" he shouted in a fine proud voice, a little husky, and everybody cheered. All I could hear was the cheering and yipping all around me, but I could see his eyes light up and his mouth moving the way it will do when a man is using big words. I thought I heard something about defenders and liberty and even something about the women back home but I couldnt be sure; there was so much racket. When he was through he stood in the stirrups, raising his cap to us as we went by, and I recognized him. It was General Beauregard, the man I'd come to fight for, and I hadnt hardly heard a word he said.

We stayed lined up better now because we were through the worst of the briers and vines, but just as we got going good there was a terrible clatter off to the right, the sound of firecrackers mixed with a roaring and yapping like a barn full of folks at a Fourth of July dogfight or a gouging match. The line begun to crook and weave because some of the men had stopped to listen, and Captain Plummer was cussing them, tongue-tied. Joe Marsh was next to me—he was nearly thirty, middle-aged, and had seen some battle up near Bowling Green. "There you are," he said, slow and calm and proud of himself. "Some outfit has met the elephant." That was what the ones who had been in action always called it: the elephant.

They had told us how it would be. They said we would march two days and on the third day we would hit them where they were camped between two creeks with their backs to the Tennessee River. We would drive them, the colonel told us, and when they were pushed against the river we would kill or capture the whole she-bang. I didnt understand it much because what the colonel said was full of tactics talk. Later the captain explained it, and that was better but not much. So then Sergeant Tyree showed it to us by drawing lines on the ground with a stick. That way it was clear as could be.

It sounded fine, the way he told it; it sounded simple and easy. Maybe it was too simple, or something. Anyhow things didnt turn out so good when it came to doing them. On the third day we were still marching, all day, and here it was the fourth day and we were still just marching, stop and go but mostly stop—the only real difference was that the column was moving sideways now, through the woods instead of on the road. From all that racket over on the right I thought maybe the other outfits would have the Yankees pushed back and captured before we even got to see it. The noise had died down for a minute, but as we went forward it swelled up again, rolling toward the left where we were, rifles popping and popping and the soldiers yelling crazy in the distance. It didnt sound like any elephant to me.

We came clear of the woods where they ended on a ridge overlooking a valley with a little creek running through it. The ground was open all across the valley, except where the creek bottom was overgrown, and mounted to another ridge on the other side where the woods began again. There were white spots in the fringe of trees—these were tents, I made out. We were the left brigade of the whole army. The 15th Arkansas, big men mostly, with bowie knives and rolled-up sleeves, was spread across the front for skirmishers, advanced a little way in the open. There was a Tennessee regiment on our right and two more on our left and still another at the left rear with flankers out. Then we were all in the open, lined up with our flags riffling in the breeze. Colonel Thornton was out front, between us and the skirmishers. His saber flashed in the sun. Looking down the line I saw the other regimental commanders, and all their sabers were flashing sunlight too. It was like a parade just before it begins.

This is going to be what they promised us, I said to myself. This is going to be the charge.

That was when General Johnston rode up. He came right past where I was standing, a fine big man on a bay stallion. He had on a broad-brim hat and a cape and thigh boots with gold spurs that twinkled like sparks of fire. I watched him ride by, his mustache flaring out from his mouth and his eyes set deep under his forehead. He was certainly the handsomest man I ever saw, bar none; he made the other officers on his staff look small. There was a little blond-headed lieutenant bringing up the rear, the one who would go all red in the face when the men guyed him back on the march. He looked about my age, but that was the only thing about us that was alike. He had on a natty uniform: bobtail jacket, red silk neckerchief, fire-gilt buttons, and all. I said to myself, I bet his ma would have a fit if she could see him now.

General Johnston rode between our regiment and the Tennessee boys on our right, going forward to where the skirmish line was waiting. When the colonel in charge had reported, General Johnston spoke to the skirmishers: "Men of Arkansas, they say you boast of your prowess with the bowie knife. Today you wield a nobler weapon: the bayonet. Employ it well." They stood there holding their rifles and looking up at him, shifting their feet a little and looking sort of embarrassed. He was the only man I ever saw who wasnt a preacher and yet could make that high-flown way of talking sound right. Then he turned his horse and rode back through our line, and as he passed he leaned sideways in the saddle and spoke to us: "Look along your guns, and fire low." It made us ready and anxious for what was coming.

Captain Plummer walked up and down the company front. He was short, inclined to fat, and walked with a limp from the blisters he developed on the march. "Stay dwessed on me, wherever I go," he said.

"And shoot low. Aim for their knees." All up and down the line the flags were flapping and other officers were speaking to their men.

I was watching toward the front, where we would go, but all I could see was that empty valley with the little creek running through it and the rising ground beyond ,with the trees on top. While I was looking, trying hard to see was anybody up there, all of a sudden there was a Boom! Boom! Boom! directly in the rear and it scared me so bad I almost broke for cover. But when I looked around I saw they had brought up the artillery and it was shooting over our heads towards the left in a shallow swale. I felt real sheepish from having jumped but when I looked around I saw that the others had jumped as much as I had, and now they were joking at one another about who had been the most scared, carrying it off all brave-like but looking kind of hang-dog about it too. I was still trying to see whatever it was out front that the artillery was shooting at, but all I could see was that valley with the creek in it and the dark trees on the flanks.

I was still mixed up, wondering what it all meant, when we begun to go forward, carrying our rifles at right shoulder shift the way we had been taught to do on parade. Colonel Thornton was still out front, flashing his saber and calling back over his shoulder:

"Close up, men. Close up. Guiiide centerrrrr!" The skirmishers went out of sight in the swale, the same as if they had marched into the ground. When we got to where they had gone down, we saw them again, but closer now, kneeling and popping little white puffs of smoke from their rifles. The rattle of firing rolled across the line and back again, and then it broke into just general firing. I still couldnt see what they were shooting at, specially not now that the smoke was banking up and drifting back against us with a stink like burning feathers.

Then, for the first time since we left Corinth, bugles begun to blare and it passed to the double. The line wavered like a shaken rope, gaining in places and lagging in others and all around me they were yelling those wild crazy yells. General Cleburne was on his mare to our left, between us and the 5th Tennessee. He was waving his sword and the mare was plunging and tossing her mane. I could hear him hollering the same as he would when we did wrong on the drill field—he had that thick, Irish way of speaking that came on him when he got mad. We were trotting by then.

As we went forward we caught up with the skirmishers. They had given around a place where the ground was flat and dark green and there was water in the grass, sparkling like silver. It was a bog.

We gave to the right to stay on hard ground and the 5th Tennessee gave to the left; the point of swampland was between us, growing wider as we went. General Cleburne rode straight ahead, waving his sword and bawling at us to close the gap, close the gap, and before he knew what had separated us, the mare was pastern-deep in it, floundering and bucking to get rid of the general's weight. He was waving his sword with one hand and shaking his fist at us with the other, so that when the mare gave an extra hard buck General Cleburne went flying off her nigh side and landed on his hands and knees in the mud. We could hear him cussing across two hundred yards of bog. The last I saw of him he was walking out, still waving the sword, picking his knees high and sinking almost to his boot-tops every step. His face was red as fire.

The brigade was split, two regiments on the right and four on the left, with a swamp between us; we would have to charge the high ground from two sides. By this time we had passed around where the other slope came out to a point leading down to the bog and we couldnt even see the other regiments. When we hit the rise we begun to run. I could hear Colonel Thornton puffing like a switch engine and I thought to myself, He's too old for this. Nobody was shooting yet because we didnt see anything to shoot at; we were so busy trying to keep up, we didnt have a

chance to see anything at all. The line was crooked
as a ram's horn. Some men were pushing out front
and others were beginning to breathe hard and lag
behind. My heart was hammering at my throat—it
seemed like every breath would bust my lungs. I
passed a fat fellow holding his side and groaning. At
first I thought he was shot, but then I realized he just
had a stitch. It was Burt Tapley, the one everybody
jibed about how much he ate; he was a great one for
the sutlers. Now all that fine food, canned peaches
and suchlike, was staring him in the face.

When we were halfway up the rise I begun to see
black shapes against the rim where it sloped off sharp.
At first I thought they were scarecrows—they looked
like scarecrows. That didnt make sense, except they
looked so black and stick-like. Then I saw they were
moving, wiggling, and the rim broke out with smoke,
some of it going straight up and some jetting toward
our line, rolling and jumping with spits of fire mixed
in and a humming like wasps past my ears. I thought:
Lord to God, theyre shooting; theyre shooting at me!
And it surprised me so, I stopped to look. The smoke
kept rolling up and out, rolling and rolling, still with
the stabs of fire mixed in, and some of the men passed
me, bent forward like they were running into a high
wind, rifles held crossways so that the bayonets

74

glinted and snapped in the sunlight, and their faces were all out of shape from the yelling.

When I stopped I begun to hear all sorts of things I hadnt heard while I was running. It was like being born again, coming into a new world. There was a great crash and clatter of firing, and over all this I could hear them all around me, screaming and yelping like on a foxhunt except there was something crazy mixed up in it too, like horses trapped in a burning barn. I thought theyd all gone crazy—they looked it, for a fact. Their faces were split wide open with screaming, mouths twisted every which way, and this wild lunatic yelping coming out. It wasnt like they were yelling with their mouths: it was more like the yelling was something pent up inside them and they were opening their mouths to let it out. That was the first time I really knew how scared I was.

If I'd stood there another minute, hearing all this, I would have gone back. I thought: Luther, you got no business mixed up in all this ruckus. This is all crazy, I thought. But a big fellow I never saw before ran into me full tilt, knocking me forward so hard I nearly went sprawling. He looked at me sort of desperate, like I was a post or something that got in the way, and went by, yelling. By the time I got my balance I was stumbling forward, so I just kept going. And that was better. I found that as long as I was moving I was all right, because then I didnt hear so much or even see so much. Moving, it was more like I was off to myself, with just my own particular worries.

I kept passing men lying on the ground, and at first I thought they were winded, like the fat one—that was the way they looked to me. But directly I saw a corporal with the front of his head mostly gone, what had been under his skull spilling over his face, and I knew they were down because they were hurt. Every now and then there would be one just sitting there holding an arm or leg and groaning. Some of them would reach out at us and even call us by name, but we stayed clear. For some reason we didnt like them, not even the sight of them. I saw Lonny Parker that I grew up with; he was holding his stomach, bawling like a baby, his face all twisted and big tears on his cheeks. But it wasnt any different with Lonny—I stayed clear of him too, just like I'd never known him, much less grown up with him back in Jordan County. It wasnt a question of luck, the way some folks will tell you; they will tell you it's bad luck to be near the wounded. It was just that we didnt want to be close to them any longer than it took to run past, the way you wouldnt want to be near someone who had something catching, like smallpox.

We were almost to the rim by then and I saw

clear enough that they werent scarecrows—that was a foolish thing to think anyhow. They were men, with faces and thick blue uniforms. It was only a glimpse, though, because then we gave them a volley and smoke rolled out between us. When we came through the smoke they were gone except the ones who were on the ground. They lay in every position, like a man I saw once that had been drug out on bank after he was run over by a steamboat and the paddles hit him. We were running and yelling, charging across the flat ground where white canvas tents stretched out in an even row. The racket was louder now, and then I knew why. It was because I was yelling too, crazy and blood-curdled as the rest of them.

I passed one end of the row of tents. That must have been where their officers stayed, for breakfast was laid on a table there with a white cloth nice as a church picnic. When I saw the white-flour biscuits and the coffee I understood why people called them the Feds and us the Corn-feds. I got two of the biscuits (I had to grab quick; everybody was snatching at them) and while I was stuffing one in my mouth and the other in my pocket, I saw Burt Tapley. He'd caught up when we stopped to give them that volley, I reckon, and he was holding the coffee pot like a loving-cup, drinking scalding coffee in big gulps. It ran from both corners of his mouth, down onto the breast of his uniform.

Officers were running around waving their swords and hollering. "Form!" they yelled at us. "Form for attack!" But nobody paid them much mind—we were too busy rummaging the tents. So they begun to lay about with the flats of their swords, driving us away from the plunder. It didnt take long. When we were formed in line again, reloading our guns, squads and companies mixed every which way, they led us through the row of tents at a run. All around me, men were tripping on the ropes and cussing and barking their shins on the stakes. Then we got through and I saw why the officers had been yelling for us to form.

There was a gang of Federal soldiers standing shoulder to shoulder in the field beyond the tents. I thought it was the whole Yankee army, lined up waiting for us. Those in front were kneeling under the guns of the men in the second line, a great bank of blue uniforms and rifle barrels and white faces like rows of eggs, one above another. When they fired, the smoke came at us in a solid wall. Things plucked at my clothes and twitched my hat, and when I looked around I saw men all over the ground, in the same ugly positions as the men back on the slope, moaning and whimpering, clawing at the grass. Some

78

were gut-shot, making high yelping sounds like a turpentined dog.

Smoke was still thick when the second volley came. For a minute I thought I was the only one left alive. Then I saw the others through the smoke, making for the rear, and I ran too, back toward the tents and the slope where we'd come up. They gave us another volley as we ran but it was high; I could hear the balls screech over my head. I cleared the ridge on the run, and when I came over I saw them stopping. I pulled up within twenty yards or so and lay flat on the ground, panting.

No bullets were falling here but everybody laid low because they were crackling and snapping in the air over our heads on a line with the rim where our men were still coming over. They would come over prepared to run another mile, and then they would see us lying there and they would try to stop, stumbling and sliding downhill.

I saw one man come over, running sort of straddle-legged, and just as he cleared the rim I saw the front of his coat jump where the shots came through. He was running down the slope, stone dead already, the way a deer will do when it's shot after picking up speed. This man kept going for nearly fifty yards downhill before his legs stopped pumping and he crashed into the ground on his stomach. I could see his

face as he ran, and there was no doubt about it, no
doubt at all: he was dead and I could see it in his face.

That scared me worse than anything up to then.
It wasnt really all that bad, looking back on it: it
was just that he'd been running when they shot
him and his drive kept him going down the slope.
But it seemed so wrong, so scandalous, somehow so
un*religious* for a dead man to have to keep on fighting
—or running, anyhow—that it made me sick at my
stomach. I didnt want to have any more to do with
the war if this was the way it was going to be.

They had told us we would push them back to
the river. Push, they said; that was the word they
used. I really thought we were going to push them—
with bullets and bayonets of course, and of course I
knew there were going to be men killed: I even
thought I might get killed myself; it crossed my mind
a number of times. But it wasnt the way they said.
It wasnt that way at all. Because even the dead and
dying didnt have any decency about them—first the
Yankees back on the slope, crumpled and muddy
where their own men had overrun them, then the
men in the field beyond the tents, yelping like gut-
shot dogs while they died, and now this one, this
big fellow running straddle-legged and stone cold
dead in the face, that wouldnt stop running even after
he'd been killed.

I was what you might call unnerved, for they may warn you there's going to be bleeding in battle but you dont believe it till you see the blood. What happened from then on was all mixed up in the smoke. We formed again and went back through the tents. But the same thing happened: they were there, just as before, and when they threw that wall of smoke and humming bullets at us, we came running back down the slope. Three times we went through and it was the same every time. Finally a fresh brigade came up from the reserve and we went through together.

This trip was different—we could tell it even before we got started. We went through the smoke and the bullets, and that was the first time we used bayonets. For a minute it was jab and slash, everyone yelling enough to curdle your blood just with the shrillness. I was running, bent low with the rifle held out front, the way they taught me, and all of a sudden I saw I was going to have it with a big Yank wearing his coat unbuttoned halfway, showing a red flannel undershirt. I was running and he was waiting, braced, and it occurred to me, the words shooting through my mind: What kind of a man is this, would wear a red wool undershirt in April?

I saw his face from below, but he had bent down and his eyebrows were drawn in a straight line like a black bar over his eyes. He was full-grown, with a wide brown mustache; I could see the individual hairs on each side of the shaved line down the middle. I'd have had to say Sir to him back home. Then something hit my arm a jar—I stumbled against him, lifting my rifle and falling sideways. Ee! I'm killed! I thought. He turned with me and we were falling, first a slow fall the way it is in dreams, then sudden, and the ground came up and hit me: ho! We were two feet apart, looking at each other. He seemed even bigger now, up close, and there was something wrong with the way he looked. Then I saw why.

My bayonet had gone in under his jaw, the hand-guard tight against the bottom of his chin, and the point must have stuck in his head bone because he appeared to be trying to open his mouth but couldnt. It was like he had a mouthful of something bitter and couldnt spit—his eyes were screwed up, staring at me and blinking a bit from the strain. All I could do was look at him; I couldnt look away, no matter how I tried. A man will look at something that is making him sick but he cant stop looking until he begins to vomit —something holds him. That was the way it was with me. Then, while I was watching him, this fellow reached up and touched the handle of the bayonet under his chin. He touched it easy, using the tips of his fingers, tender-like. I could see he wanted to grab and pull it out but he was worried about how much it would hurt and he didnt dare.

I let go of the rifle and rolled away. There were bluecoats running across the field and through the woods beyond. All around me men were kneeling and shooting at them like rabbits as they ran. Captain Plummer and two lieutenants were the only officers left on their feet. Two men were bent over Colonel Thornton where they had propped him against a tree with one of his legs laid crooked. Captain Plummer wasnt limping now—he'd forgotten his blisters, I reckon. He wasnt even hurt, so far as I could see, but the skirt of his coat was ripped where somebody had taken a swipe at him with a bayonet or a saber.

He went out into the open with a man carrying the colors, and then begun to wave his sword and call in a high voice: "6th Mississippi, wally here! 6th Mississippi, wally here!"

Men begun straggling over, collecting round the flag, so I got up and went over with them. We were a sorry lot. My feet were so heavy I could barely lift them, and I had to carry my left arm with my right, the way a baby would cradle a doll. The captain kept calling, "Wally here! 6th Mississippi, wally here!" but after a while he saw there werent any more to rally so he gave it up. There were a little over a hundred of us, all that were left out of the four hundred and twenty-five that went in an hour before.

Our faces were gray, the color of ashes. Some had powder burns red on their cheeks and foreheads and running back into singed patches in their hair. Mouths were rimmed with grime from biting cartridges, mostly a long smear down one corner, and hands were blackened with burnt powder off the ramrods. We'd aged a lifetime since the sun came up. Captain Plummer was calling us to rally, rally here, but there wasnt much rally left in us. There wasnt much left in me, anyhow. I felt so tired it was all I could do to make it to where the flag was. I was worried, too, about not having my rifle. I remembered what Sergeant Tyree was always saying: "Your rifle is your best friend. Take care of it." But if that meant pulling it out of the man with the mustache, it would just have to stay there. Then I looked down and be durn if there wasnt one just like it at my feet. I picked it up, stooping and nursing my bad arm, and stood there with it.

Joe Marsh was next to me. At first I didnt know him. He didnt seem bad hurt, but he had a terrible look around the eyes and there was a knot on his forehead the size of a walnut where some Yank had bopped him with a rifle butt. I thought to ask him how the Tennessee breed of elephant compared with the Kentucky breed, but I didnt. He looked at me, first in the face till he finally recognized me, then down at my arm.

"You better get that tended to."

"It dont hurt much," I said.

"All right. Have it your way."

He didnt pay me any mind after that. He had lorded it over me for a month about being a green-horn, yet here I was, just gone through meeting as big an elephant as any he had met, and he was still trying the same high-and-mightiness. He was mad now because he wasnt the only one who had seen some battle. He'd had his big secret to throw up to us, but not any more. We all had it now.

We were milling around like ants when their hill is upset, trying to fall-in the usual way, by platoons and squads, but some were all the way gone and others had only a couple of men. So we gave that up and just fell-in in three ranks, not even making a good-sized company. Captain Plummer went down the line, looking to see who was worst hurt. He looked at the way I was holding my arm. "Bayonet?"

"Yes sir."

"Cut you bad?"

"It dont hurt much, captain. I just cant lift it no higher than this."

He looked me in the face, and I was afraid he

85

thought I was lying to keep from fighting any more. "All wight," he said. "Fall out and join the others under that twee."

There were about two dozen of us under it when he got through, including some that hadnt been able to get in ranks in the first place. They were hacked up all kinds of ways. One had lost an ear and he was the worst worried man of the lot; "Does it look bad?" he kept asking, wanting to know how it would seem to the folks back home. We sat under the tree and watched Captain Plummer march what was left of the regiment away. They were a straggly lot. We were supposed to wait there under the tree till the doctor came.

We waited, hearing rifles clattering and cannons booming and men yelling further and further in the woods, and the sun climbed up and it got burning hot. I could look back over the valley where we had charged. It wasnt as wide as it had been before. There were men left all along the way, lying like bundles of dirty clothes. I had a warm, lazy feeling, like on a summer Sunday in the scuppernong arbor back home; next thing I knew I was sound asleep. Now that was strange. I was never one for sleeping in the daytime, not even in that quiet hour after dinner when all the others were taking their naps.

When I woke up the sun was past the overhead and

only a dozen or so of the wounded were still there. The fellow next to me (he was hurt in the leg) said they had drifted off to find a doctor. "Aint no doctor coming here," he said. "They aint studying us now we're no more good to them." He had a flushed look, like a man in a fever, and he was mad at the whole army, from General Johnston down to me.

My arm was stiff and the blood had dried on my sleeve. There was just a slit where the bayonet blade went in. It felt itchy, tingling in all directions from the cut, like the spokes of a wheel, but I still hadnt looked at it and I wasnt going to. All except two of the men under the tree were leg wounds, not counting myself, and those two were shot up bad around the head. One was singing a song about the bells of Tennessee but it didnt make much sense.

"Which way did they go?"

"Ever which way," one said.

"Yonder ways, mostly," another said, and pointed over to the right. The shooting was a long way off now, loudest toward the right front. It seemed reasonable that the doctors would be near the loudest shooting.

I thought I would be dizzy when I stood up but I felt fine, light on my feet and tingly from not having moved for so long. I walked away nursing my arm. When I reached the edge of the field I looked back.

They were spread around the tree trunk, sprawled out favoring their wounds. I could hear that crazy one singing the Tennessee song.

I walked on, getting more and more light-headed, till finally it felt like I was walking about six inches off the ground. I thought I was still asleep, dreaming, except for the ache in my arm. And I saw things no man would want to see twice. There were dead men all around, Confederate and Union, some lying where they fell and others up under bushes where theyd crawled to keep from getting trampled. There were wounded men too, lots of them, wandering around like myself, their faces dazed and pale from losing blood and being scared.

I told myself: You better lay down before you fall down. Then I said: No, youre not bad hurt; keep going. It was like an argument, two voices inside my head and neither one of them mine:

You better lay down.

—No: you feel fine.

Youll fall and theyll never find you.

—Thats not true. Youre just a little light-headed. Youll be all right.

No you wont. Youre hurt. Youre hurt worse than you think. Lay down.

They went on like that, arguing, and I followed the road, heading south by the sun until I came to a log cabin with a cross on its ridgepole and a little wooden signboard, hand-lettered: Shiloh Meeting House. It must have been some kind of headquarters now because there were officers inside, bending over maps, and messengers kept galloping up with papers.

I took a left where the road forked, and just beyond the fork there was a sergeant standing with the reins of two horses going back over his shoulder. When I came up he looked at me without saying anything.

"Where is a doctor?" I asked him. My voice sounded strange from not having used it for so long.

"I dont know, bud," he said. But he jerked his thumb down the road toward the sound of the guns. "Should be some of them up there, back of where the fighting is." He was a Texan, by the sound of his voice; it came partly through his nose.

So I went on down the road. It had been a line of battle that morning, the dead scattered thick on both sides. I was in a fever by then, thinking crazy, and it seemed to me that all the dead men got there this way:

God was making men and every now and then He would do a bad job on one, and He would look at it and say, "This one wont do," and He would toss it in a tub He kept there, maybe not even finished with it. And finally, 6 April 1862, the tub got full and God emptied it right out of heaven and they landed here, along this road, tumbled down in all positions, some without arms and legs, some with their heads and bodies split open where they hit the ground so hard.

I was in a fever bad, to think a thing like that. So there's no telling how long I walked or how far, but I know I came near covering that battlefield from flank to flank. It must have been a couple of hours and maybe three miles, but far as I was concerned it could have been a year and a thousand miles. At first all I wanted was a doctor. Finally I didnt even want that. All I wanted was to keep moving. I had an idea if I stopped I wouldnt be able to start again. That kept me going.

I didnt notice much along the way, but once I passed an open space with a ten-acre peach orchard in bloom at the far end and cannons puffing smoke up through the blossoms. Great crowds of men were trying to reach the orchard—they would march up in long lines and melt away; there would be a pause and then other lines would march up and melt away. Then I was past all this, in the woods again, and I came to a little gully where things were still and peaceful, like in another world almost; the guns seemed far away. That was the place for me to stop, if any place was. I sat down, leaning back against a stump, and all the weariness came down on me at once. I knew I wouldnt get up then, not even if I could, but I didnt mind.

I didnt mind anything. It was like I was somewhere outside myself, looking back. I had reached the stage where a voice can tell you it is over, youre going to die, and that is all right too. Dying is as good as living, maybe better. The main thing is to be left alone, and if it takes dying to be let alone, a man thinks: All right, let me die. He thinks: Let me die, then.

This gully was narrow and deep, really a little valley, less than a hundred yards from ridge to ridge. The trees were thick but I could see up to the crest in each direction. There were some dead men and some wounded scattered along the stream that ran through, but I think they must have crawled in after water—there hadnt been any fighting here and there werent any bullets in the trees. I leaned back against the stump, holding my arm across my lap and facing the forward ridge. Then I saw two horsemen come over, side by side, riding close together, one leaning against the other. The second had his arm around the first, holding him in the saddle.

The second man was in civilian clothes, a boxback coat and a wide black hat. It was Governor Harris; I used to see him when he visited our brigade to talk to the Tennessee boys—electioneering, he called it; he was the Governor of Tennessee. The first man had his head down, reeling in the saddle, but I could see the braid on his sleeves and the wreath of stars on his collar. Then he lolled the other way, head rolling, and I saw him full in the face. It was General Johnston.

His horse was shot up, wounded in three legs, and his uniform had little rips in the cape and trouser-legs where minie balls had nicked him. One bootsole flapped loose, cut crossways almost through. In his right hand he held a tin cup, one of his fingers still hooked through the handle. I heard about the cup afterwards—he got it earlier in the day. He was riding through a captured camp and one of his lieutenants came out of a Yank colonel's tent and showed him a fine brier pipe he'd found there. General Johnston said "None of that, Sir. We are not here for plunder." Then he must have seen he'd hurt the lieutenant's feelings, for he leaned down from his horse and picked up this tin cup off a table and said, "Let this be my share of the spoils today," and used it instead of a sword to direct the battle.

They came down the ridge and stopped under a big oak at the bottom, near where I was, and Governor Harris got off between the horses and eased the general down to the ground. He began to ask questions, trying to make him answer, but he wouldnt —couldnt. He undid the general's collar and unfastened his clothes, trying to find where he was shot, but he couldnt find it. He took out a bottle and tried to make him drink (it was brandy; I could smell it) but he wouldnt swallow, and when Governor Harris turned his head the brandy ran out of his mouth.

Then a tall man, wearing the three stars of a colonel, came hurrying down the slope, making straight for where General Johnston was laid out on the ground. He knelt down by his side, leaning forward so that their faces were close together, eye to eye, and begun to nudge him on the shoulder and speak to him in a shaky voice: "Johnston, do you know me? Johnston, do you know me?"

But the general didnt know him; the general was dead. He still looked handsome, lying there with his eyes glazing over.

4 *Private Otto Flickner*
Cannoneer, 1st Minnesota Battery

He would have reached about to my chin if he'd stood up, but he wouldnt; he just sat there. When I asked him to rise and take his punishment for calling me a coward, he said: "If youre so allfired brave, sonny, what you doing back here with us skulkers then?"

"I aint scared the way you made out," I said. "I'm what they call demoralized."

"Yair?"

"It's just I lost my confidence."

"Yair?" He kept saying that.

"Get up here, I'll show you."

But he wouldnt. He just sat there hugging his knees and looking at me with a lop-sided grin on his face. "If what you want's a fight, go up the bluff. Thats where the fighting is." Then he said, still grinning:

97

"Ive already showed the whole wide world *I'm* yellow."

I intended to jump him, sitting or no, but what can you do when a man talks like that? saying right out in front of God and everybody that he's scared; it would be the same as fighting something you found when you picked up a rotted log. The others thought it was fun, guffawed at hearing him talk that way. They could laugh about it now—they had got used to being scared and now they made jokes about it.

They would come down from above looking shame-faced but after a while, when theyd been down here an hour, theyd brighten up and begin to bluster, bragging about how long they held their ground before they broke. "Ive done *my* part," theyd say, wagging their heads. But they were all thinking the selfsame thing: *I might be a disgrace to my country. I might be a coward, even. But I'm not up there in those woods getting shot at.*

And I must admit I had it reasoned the same way. You would form at the warning and get set for some honest fighting, stand up and slug, and theyd come squalling that wild crazy yell—not even human, hardly—and you would stand there at the guns throwing solid shot, then canister and grape, holding them good. And then, sure enough, word would come to bring up the horses: it was time to retire to

98

a new position because some paddle-foot outfit on your left or right was giving way and you had to fall back to keep from getting captured. Twice was all right—you thought maybe that was the way it was supposed to be. But three times was once too often. Men began to walk away, making for the rear. When Lieutenant Pfaender called to them to stand-to theyd just keep walking, not even looking round. So finally, after the third time, I walked too. So much is enough but a little bit more is too much.

There were ten thousand of us under the bluff before the day was through (—thats the number I heard told and I believe it) —some scrunched down on the sand where the bluff reared up a hundred feet in the air, others going along the riverbank downstream to where they could wade or swim the creek and get away. "I killed as many of them as they did of me," some said, and laughed. All the time there was this thumping of guns and this ripping sound of rifles from up above, and every now and then the rebel cheering would get louder when they took another camp.

We were all ranks down here, though you couldnt tell just which in most cases because they had torn off their chevrons and shoulder straps and all you could see was the broken threads that had held them on. In some cases you couldnt even tell that, for theyd even picked the threads out, those that had the time. But that didnt work either because you could still see the darker patches where the sun and rain had weathered the cloth around the place where theyd been sewed.

They made a complaint, blaming their officers and telling how the lieutenants and captains didnt know any more about soldiering than the privates. When they first came down they would keep their backs turned, not speaking to anybody, still trembling from the scare. But after a while theyd look around and begin to feel better. Then they would start talking, just a little at first, sort of feeling the others out, then all together, every man trying to tell his story at the same time. They collected in groups of anywhere from three to thirty, hunkered up side by side and talking or just sitting there looking to see who they could recognize in the crowd. When they saw somebody they knew, their eyes would say: *If you wont tell on me I wont on you*, but not out loud.

There were five in the group I joined, not counting the dog. The man that had him said he was a Tennessee hound, a redbone, but he looked more like a Tennessee walking-horse. At first I thought he was shot up bad: there was clotted blood and patches of torn skin all over his hide. But the fellow said he wasnt even scratched. "He's demoralized—like you," the fellow said, grinning. Then he told how it happened.

"I was on Guard last night," he said. He had that Ohio way of talking, bearing down hard on the R's. "We come off post at four and went to our bunks at the back of the guard tent. Just before dawn my Tennessee quickstep signaled me a hurry-up call for the bushes, and when I went out I saw the officer of the day (Captain Fountain, from up at Regimental) sitting at the table out front, writing a letter by lamplight. The dog was at his feet, asleep, but when I went past he raised his head and looked at me with those big round yellow eyes, then dropped his jaw back on his paws and went to sleep again. When I come back he didnt even look up. He was our mascot, knew every man in the 53d by sight. We named him Bango the day he joined up. —Well, I woke up it was daylight and all outside the tent there was a racket and a booming. 'Thats cannon,' I said to myself, still half asleep; 'we're attackted!' and grabbed my gun and started for the front of the tent. But there was a terrible bang and a flash before I got there, smoke enough to blind you. It cleared some then and I saw what had happened. A rebel shell had come through the tent fly and landed square on top of Captain Fountain. It went off in his lap before he had time to so much as know what hit him. There wasnt much of him left.

It blew blood and guts all over the dog, scared him so bad he wasnt even howling—he was just laying there making little whimpering sounds, bloody as a stuck hog, trembling all over and breathing in shallow pants. I went out and formed with the others. But soon as Colonel Appler seen the johnnies coming across the field, he got down behind a log and hollered: 'Retreat! *Save* yourselves!' Well, I know a sensible order when I hear one, and if anybody asks me what I'm doing back here, I'll say I'm where my colonel sent me. Which is more than most of you can say.—On the way to the rear I passed the guard tent again and there was Bango the same as before, laying there whimpering with the captain's blood all over him. So I brought him back here with me to see could he get himself together again. But he dont seem to be doing so good, does he?"

He reached down and stroked the dog on the muzzle, but Bango didnt pay him any heed. He just lay there, belly close to the sand, breathing quick little breaths up high in his throat, eyes all rimmed with red. I could see his hide quiver under the dried blood.

I said, "Whynt you take him down to the river and wash him off?"

"Well, I dont know," the Ohio man said. "I think

maybe if he gets another shock he might start snapping."

Seeing the size of those jaws, I couldnt blame him. After all, when you came right down to it, he was a Rebel dog anyhow. There was no telling *what* he'd do.

The other three men had told their stories, and they were all three pretty much the same. They told how they had stayed in line and fought till they saw it was no use staying, and went. I told how it had been with me, how I hung on till things came to pieces that third time, and then walked off the same as the others had done. I told them what Sergeant Buterbaugh had said about the men that were walking away, that they werent necessarily cowards; they were just demoralized from losing their confidence. That was when this Michigander said it was all hogwash. We were *all* cowards back here, he said—and then wouldnt get up and fight.

When it began we were in position on the right of the Corinth road at the edge of a strip of woods where our tents were pitched. There was a big open field on the left of the road. Captain Hickenlooper's Ohio battery was advanced into the field. The infantry was in camp along our front and some more were in our rear. We'd been there two days.

At three oclock that morning I lay warm in my

blankets and heard the advance party going out on a scout. I knew the time for I took out granddaddy's watch and looked at it. This party was going out because General Prentiss had had a feeling all the day before that something spooky was going on out front. I went back to sleep then, feeling glad I was in the artillery and didnt have to be up beating the bushes for rebs at blue oclock in the morning. Almost before I had time to know I was asleep I heard them coming back and the long roll sounding.

By sunup we were posted at the guns, watching the infantry come past. They had a serious look on their faces but they still could joke with us. "You easy-living boys had better get set," they said. "There's johnnies out there thicker than fleas on a billy goat in a barnlot."

We didnt see them, though, for a long time. This was what we'd been training for all those weeks of rollcall and drill, greasing caissons and gun carriages, tending the horses and standing inspection, cleaning limber chests and sorting ammunition. We were downright glad it had come, and all the fellows began making jokes at one another about who was going to funk it. The Hickenlooper boys would call over to us, wanting to know how Minnesota was feeling today, and we'd call back, telling them theyd better be worrying about Ohio; Minnesota was all right; Minnesota could take care of herself.

All this time there was a ruckus over on the right. It rolled back and forth, getting louder and more furious with yelling mixed up in it. But still they didnt come. We kept expecting word to limber and move in the direction of the firing. We didnt like it, waiting that way. It was the same old story—hurry up; wait —while the sound of the shooting swelled and died and swelled again. Everybody began asking questions:

"Aint they coming this way, Butterball?"

"Yair, sergeant: when are they coming *this* way?"

"Bide your time," he said. "Theyll be here all right."

"I wish if they was coming theyd come on."

"Theyll be here," Sergeant Buterbaugh said.

He was a college man, up for a commission, and to tell the truth I never liked him. But he had a way of saying things—he knew all the stars, for instance, and could tell you their names.

Sure enough, soon as the words were out of his mouth the infantry began popping away and smoke began lazing up from the bushes out front. I couldnt see what they were shooting at. Far as I could tell, they were banging away at nothing to keep themselves amused the way pickets sometimes do. Captain Munch walked up and down, going from gun to gun and saying, "Steady. Steady, men," like he thought we might take a notion to go into a dance or something. We stood at cannoneers' posts, ready to fire whenever he gave us a target. I was on the handspike because of my size. Then the firing stepped up. Smoke began to roll and drift back against us. There was a high yipping sound somewhere out in front of the smoke, like a cage full of beagles at feeding time.

They didnt come the way I thought at all. I thought it would be the same as on parade, long lines of men marching with their flags spanking the wind, sleeves and pants legs flapping in cadence, and us standing at our posts the way it was in gun drill, mowing them down. But they didnt come like that. They came in driblets, scattered all across the front and through the woods, no two of them moving the same way, running from bush to bush like mice or rabbits. No sooner I'd see a man than he would be gone again. The only thing that stayed put was the smoke—it boiled up a dirty gray and rolled along the ground with little stabs of yellow and pink flicking in it where the muzzles flashed. There was a humming in the air like in the orchard back home when the bees swarmed, only more so.

But Captain Munch began to sing out commands, and from then on it was hot work, ram and prime and touch her off, roll her back and load again. All six guns were going full time, throwing big balls of fire and smoke out over the battery front, and we were cheering while we fired. I couldnt see it very well but the captain was bringing us in on a regiment drawn up at the far end of the field. We had the range, about a thousand yards, and we could see the flags go down fluttering and the men milling around while the balls chewed up their ranks.

During a pause, while I stood at the trail and the rest were out front swabbing the bore, I looked over to the right and saw the gun in the next platoon lying on its side, one of its wheels splintered to the hub and the other one canted up at an angle. I couldnt think what had done that to it, except maybe a premature, when all of a sudden the ground between the two guns flicked up, throwing dirt at me the way water would splash if you slapped it with a plank, and when I opened my eyes there was a little trench scooped out, about eight inches wide and maybe half that deep, and I knew what did it. Nothing but a cannonball did that—there must be a rebel battery ranging in on us. But if I wasnt sure then I knew it soon after, for here came another one and I saw it coming: a ricochet—it bounced along, whooing and bouncing, hitting the ground every twenty feet or so. I got the wild idea it somehow had a mind of its own.

Thats coming *my* way, I thought. That one's for *me*.

But it struck in front, took an extra hard bounce, and sailed right over the gun, exactly down the line of the tube and the trail—I could almost feel it in my hair. It made a whuffing sound going over; I could see the fuze lobbing around on one side of it, sputtering. I looked to see where it was going and saw it go past Captain Munch on the bounce, spinning him around sideways like a man hit by a runaway horse, and go on into the woods, rooting and banging the trees till it went off with a big orange-colored flash, the fragments singing, clipping leaves and twigs. Captain Munch just laid there and directly some men ran over and picked him up and carried him off to one side.

Then there were infantry running between the guns. Some looked back over their shoulders every now and then as they ran, but most of them had their heads down, going hard for the rear without their rifles. Their faces were pale as paper, their eyes kind of wild-looking, like a child's when you say Boo at him coming round a corner. There were horses mixed up in it (I had forgot there were horses in war; it seemed all wrong) and Sergeant Buterbaugh had me by the arm, shaking me, and I could see his mouth moving but the words did not get through. The horses kicked and plunged and I saw what it was. They were limbering for a displacement. I snagged a caisson getting under way and held on tight while it jounced and rattled across the furrows of a field. I was so busy trying to stay on (—we lost two that way; they flew off, arms outstretched like big birds, and landed in the dust, not making a sound) I didnt see where we were going. Next thing I knew, we were off to the side of the road preparing for action again, only this time we had four guns instead of six and now Lieutenant Pfaender was battery commander.

"Action rear!" Sergeant Buterbaugh was yelling. The horses were lathered and blown. "Action rear!"

But it was the same thing again, the same identical business. By the time we got off a few rounds, the infantry began passing us with that scared look on their faces. And there was the same mixup when the johnnies got our range. The horses came plunging up with the bits in their teeth, and then we were limbered and off again. The only real difference was that this time we didnt lose any guns or men. It seemed that just when we got set to do some good, word came down to clear out or be captured.

The third position was different. It was near midday by then and General Prentiss had drawn the whole division in a line along an old sunken road that wound through the woods. What was left of our battery was split in two, one section two hundred yards beyond the other, both just in rear of the road and the line of infantry. They had their dander up now, they said; they didnt intend to give up any more ground. Every man built a little pile of cartridges beside him and lay down in the sunken road with his rifle up on the shoulder. "Let 'em come on *now*," they said, talking through their gritted teeth. Their mouths were set kind of rigid-like but there was still a worried look around their eyes. I wondered if they meant it.

They meant it. We were there four hours, and surely that was the hardest fighting of this or any war. This time it was almost the way I had imagined it would be. They came at us in rows, flags flapping and everything, and we stood to our guns and cut them down. When we gave them a volley, rifles and cannon, their line would shake and weave from end to end like a wounded snake, and they would come on, trampling the blackberry bushes until we thought this time they were coming right over us, but then they would break and fall back over their dead and there would be a lull, but not for long, and they would come at us again. It didnt seem to me that they were men like us, not only because of the way they were dressed (they wore all kinds of uniforms; some even had on white—we called these their graveyard clothes) but mostly because of the way they wouldnt stop. They took killing better than any natural men would ever do, and they had a way of yelling that didnt sound even partly human, high and quavery, away up in their throats, without any brain behind it.

After we had been there three-four hours I began to notice that the gun was harder and harder to roll back into position. Fighting like that, you expected casualties. But then I saw that all the missing ones werent leaving because theyd been wounded. A man would stand there during a lull and there would be something come over his face like you see on the faces of children just before they bust out crying—sort of bulged around the mouth and shifty-eyed—and then he would start walking, not even looking round, not paying any attention to anyone that called out to him. He was heading for the rear; he'd had enough. He'd had enough and he didnt care who knew it.

Corporal Keller was cussing and calling them cowards (it was during a lull; two more had just walked off) but Sergeant Buterbaugh said no, they werent necessarily cowards; they were just demoralized from losing confidence. He was always coming out with something like that, serious, high-sounding —Butterball's jawbreakers, we called them. But this time he really hit the nail on the head. What he said stayed with me from then on, stayed in my mind, especially later when I was making for the rear myself.

I never would have done a thing like that, never in

all the world, but when word came to prepare to dis-
place again, it seemed like all the spark went out of
me. Maybe it was gone already but I think not. I was
proud of the way we'd held them—I think that did
it more than anything: to think youd done so well
and then to be told it was all for nothing. All of a
sudden I felt dog-tired, miserable.

Sergeant Buterbaugh was looking at me a peculiar
way, and I knew my face was showing the same
thing all those other faces had showed. And I began
to walk to the rear. Lieutenant Pfaender was calling
after me: "Flickner! Flickner!" but I went on, through
the blackjack scrubs. He called me again: "Flickner!
Flickner!" but I went on. I suppose by then he saw I
really meant it, the same as all the others, and then he
didnt call me any more.

My daddy took pride in telling how my granddaddy had fought against Napoleon in the old
country. It disappointed him that I never showed any
interest in such things, that I wouldnt even bother to
learn the language. I'd explain: "This is a new
country. We dont need those stories from the old
one." It seemed so wrong, so out of place, hearing
about Napoleon, when I could see right through the
living-room window the big rolling Minnesota
prairie with the tall wheat shimmering in the sunlight. But it made him sad, hearing me say that; he'd

shake his head from side to side and stroke his beard with a hurt look in his eyes, muttering German.

When I joined up and came home with the enlistment paper to show him, he took the watch and chain off the front of his vest and gave it to me, showing me how to wind it in two places, one to make it keep time and the other to make it strike the hours. Two of my brothers had already signed up and left but he hadnt given it to them. "Here," he said. "Wear this, Otto. It was your grossfather's that he wore when he went against the man you dont want I should mention. I hope you will do as well with it against this Jeffy Davis." Youd have thought it was a gun or a sword or something.

I swapped the chain for a trip down the line in St Louis and hung the watch on a string around my neck. It was safer that way anyhow. And as I went back through the woods on the way to the Landing, feeling it bump against my chest beneath my jacket, I wondered if it ever ticked off any seconds for my granddaddy when he was running from Napoleon. You think strange things when something has happened to you that you know is going to change your life. But I took some comfort remembering what Buterbaugh had said. Those men werent cowards, he said; they were just demoralized from losing confidence. And that was the way it was with me, exactly.

As I got nearer the place where the roads came together to lead down to the Landing I saw more and more men making for the rear. We had all come up this way, debarking from the transports, and we remembered that high bluff (some I suppose had been remembering it ever since the first shots fired that morning, the way it reared up a hundred feet tall between the river and the fighting) and when the going got too rough, that was the one safe place that stood out in our minds. Some had been hurt, carrying an arm buttoned into the front of their jackets or crippling along with a musket for a crutch or wearing a shirtsleeve for a bandage like a turban round their heads. Every now and again there would be a well man helping a hurt one, but generally they walked alone, not looking at the others. I got a notion they were not only trying to get away from the fighting, they were trying to walk right out of the human race.

Roads led from all corners of the battlefield up to a place on top of the bluff where they came together to form one road giving down to the Landing. We could see the water from there, steamboats at the wharf and two gunboats anchored upstream with cannons run out and sailors loafing on deck to watch the fun. The way we came together at the top of the bluff, going downhill on that one road, we were like grains of sand passing through a funnel. But that was only for a time. Once we were past this place, the spout of the funnel, we fanned out again, spreading up and down the riverbank, and sat there watching the others.

Of course I had been expecting I would find a lot of men back here—after all, I had been watching them make for the rear all day, one after another, fast as they became scared or discouraged at the way the fight was going. But I wasnt prepared for what I saw. Upstream and down, far as I could see, they crowded the space between the bluff and the bank, sitting on the sand and looking at the river, watching sunlight flash on the choppy waves and wishing like Jesus they could walk on water. A few hadnt stopped with just wishing: they were out in the river, hanging onto logs and bundles of driftwood, paddling across to the opposite bank.

It was lower over there. I could see a great mass of men drawn up in columns, waiting while some of their number—engineers, I suppose—cut a road down the low overhang so they could board the steamers. The Michigander said they were Buell's army, come from Columbia to save the day. He snorted when he said it, though, and he screwed up his eyes. "Save the day hell," he said. "Wait till they get up there. Then we'll see what they save. Theyll be right back here with the rest of us. Mind what I say. Theyll save their hides; thats all theyll save."

By the time the first boatload of them got across, it was past sundown. The sound of firing had drawn in until it seemed directly above us, on the bluff. Soon now the rebels might be looking over the rim and shooting down like into a flock of sheep. Through the fading light I watched as Buell's men came off the steamboats and onto the wharf, picking their way among the rows of wounded laid there to be taken across to safety when the chance came.

They had a hard time of it, those wounded. Retreaters had stepped on them with muddy shoes to reach the end of the wharf, in hopes that a boat might come to take the casualties across and they could crawl aboard among them. That wasnt all, either. Cables had been raked over them by the sailors, scraping some of them off into the river and fouling the rest with slime from the river bottom. You couldnt tell the dead ones from the living— theyd turned black with mud from the boots and cables and with blood from their reopened wounds. It made me sick at the stomach just looking at them.

Retreaters were packed so close where the steamboats put in, Buell's men had to open a path with their bayonets. They cussed the men on the bank, calling them scoundrels and cowards while they shoved them aside with their rifles.

"Get out the way," they said, shoving. "We'll fight your damned battle for you."

But the men under the bluff jeered right back. "*You*ll catch it," they hollered, all of them yelling at once. "*You*ll see! Theyll cut you to ribbons up there!"

Mostly we had been let alone. Not even the high-rank officers on Grant's staff, moving along the bluff road to and from Army headquarters on a steamboat, made any try at getting us back into the fight. They would just look at us and go on. I suppose they knew that even if they managed to get us back up the bluff and into the wood again, we would melt away as soon as they turned their heads. Or maybe they figured being scared was catching and they didnt want us up there spreading it amongst the men who had held.

But there was one fellow who didnt feel that way about it. He was a chaplain, tall and raw-boned, and he ranted at us in a hard New England voice. Youd have thought he was back in the pulpit, the way he ranted. He stood in the middle of the road, halfway up the bluff, waving his arms at a group of men who sat on the sand and watched him with leers on their faces. Then the head of a column of Buell's men off the steamboat came up to where he was.

"Rally for God and country!" he was saying. "Oh rally round the flag!"

He was square in the middle of the road, blocking it and calling the skulkers to rally oh rally, when the colonel heading the column came up behind him.

"Shut up, you goddam old fool," the colonel said. "Get out the way!"

And the column brushed him aside and went up the bluff while the group of skulkers sat there laughing at the parson and calling him to rally oh rally, rally. They whistled and hooted at him till he stomped off fuming mad and didnt come back.

Night was closing in, first a blue dusk darkening, then just blackness, the big stretch of sky across the river sprinkled with stars winking at us through rifts in the smoke blown back from the battlefield. The firing had died to occasional sputters, sounding dull in the darkness, but every ten or fifteen minutes the gunboats would throw two shells up over the bluff. They went past with a noise like freight cars in the night, their fuzes drawing long curved lines across the sky. The explosions sounded faint and far in the woods above, the way it is back home when a farmer two fields off is blowing stumps.

Torches were burning down by the Landing where Buell's men were still unloading. They came up the bluff in a steady column, cheering with hoarse voices when they reached the top. Nobody hooted at them now. We just sat there watching them. Their faces looked strange in the torchlight, eyes glinting out of hollow sockets, teeth flashing white against mouths like deep black holes when they cheered. From sundown until the stars burned clear with no smoke to fog them, Buell's men went on unloading and marching up that steep road to the woods above. When they reached the overlook, they would put their caps on the tips of their bayonets and raise them, cheering. Out over the water we heard the voices of the sailors as they took the steamboats across again, going back for more.

Then the stars went out and the sky across the river was only blackness. There began to be a sound of sighing in the air—the wind was rising. Then the rain came. First it was only a patter, little gusts of it as if somebody up on the bluff was dropping handfuls of birdshot down on us. Then the wind died; the rain turned to a steady, fine drizzle almost like mist. You could see it against the torches, falling slantwise on the men marching up the slope and the retreaters huddled on the sand with their faces to the bluff and their backs to the rain.

Sitting there getting wetter and wetter I began to think about the long day that was past. I saw it from then to now; I went back over it, beginning with three oclock in the morning when I lay warm in my blankets and heard the infantry going out, then back to sleep again and the long roll sounding and we stood to the guns, anxious for the johnnies to come because we still didnt know what it was going to be like. I saw Captain Munch getting bowled over by a cannon-ball. I looked at myself in my mind, watching myself as if I was another person—God, maybe—looking down and seeing Otto Flickner fighting the rebels on Shiloh battlefield.

He did all right, considering. He was scared from time to time, no different from the others, but he did all right until word came down to retreat from the sunken road. That broke it. That was when the spark went out of him. I heard Lieutenant Pfaender calling Flickner! Flickner! and saw myself going back through the blackjack scrubs without even looking round. I saw again the things I'd seen at the Landing, the hangdog faces of the skulkers turning to jeer, the wounded laid out in rows on the wharf all bloody, muddy from being tramped on; Buell's army coming off the steamboats, calling us cowards to our faces—and us taking it; and finally I saw myself the way I was now, sitting in the rain and telling myself that Buterbaugh was wrong. I wasnt demoralized back there at the sunken road: I hadnt even lost confidence. I was just plain scared, as scared as a man can be, and that was why I walked away from the fight.

Just thinking it, I was panting like the dog. And

soon as I thought it—You were just plain scared, I thought—I wished I had let it alone. Because being demoralized or losing confidence was all right. Like Buterbaugh said, it was a thing that closed in on you from outside, a thing you couldnt help. But being scared was different. It was inside you, just you yourself, and that was a horse of a different color. That meant I would have to do something about it, or live with it for the balance of my life. So I went up the bluff.

I didnt say anything to the others, and only the Michigander looked up as I walked away. I thought maybe it would be a good idea to take a poke at him before I left, but what was the use after all? Bango was sleeping—anyhow he hadnt moved. The rain was coming down harder now; when I cleared the top of the bluff it came against me in sheets, driven by the wind, and there was a steady moaning sound in the limbs of the trees. Then I saw campfires. They followed a ridge and overlooked a gully, drawing a wide low half-mile semicircle against the night. Siege guns, big ones long and black against the firelight, were ranged along that ridge with their muzzles reaching out toward the rebel lines. Later I heard that a colonel by the name of Webster—he was on Grant's staff—had placed them there, and with the help of some of the light artillery and rallied infantry, they formed the line that broke the final charge that evening. But I didnt know this now; I just saw the siege guns against the campfires strung out along the ridge.

Then I passed a log house with lanterns burning and wounded men lying half-naked on sawhorse tables, being held down by attendants while the surgeons worked on them. The surgeons wore their sleeves rolled up, arms bloody past the elbows; from time to time one would stop and take a pull at a bottle. The wounded screamed like women, high and trembly, and the attendants had to hold them tight to keep them from bucking off the tables.

I went past in a hurry, picking my way among those laid out to wait their turn in the house. It was pitch black dark and the rain was coming down harder, blowing up for a storm. Everywhere I went there were men on the ground, singly or in groups, and most of them sleeping. But no matter who I asked, not a one of them could tell me how to find my outfit.

"Where will I find the 1st Minnesota Battery?"

"Never heard of them." That was always the answer.

Once I saw a man huddled in a poncho, leaning back against the trunk of a big oak. But when I went over to ask him, I saw his face and backed away. He could have told me, maybe, but I didnt ask him. It was General Grant. He had that same worried look on his face, only more so. Earlier he'd tried to get some sleep in the log house where I saw the surgeons, but the screams of the wounded and the singing of the bone-saws drove him out into the rain. Remembering all I saw when I went past—surgeons with their sleeves rolled high and bloody arms and legs thrown in a pile outside an open window—I couldnt say I blamed him.

It went on that way: "Never heard of them," until finally I gave up trying to locate the battery. I thought I'd better find the division first; then maybe I could find the battery. But that was no better, for no one could tell me about the division either, until at last I came on a fellow leaning back in a fence corner with a blanket pulled over his head like a cowl on a monk.

"The Sixth?" he said, holding the edges of the blanket up close beneath his chin. His voice shook because his fist was against his windpipe. "Man, thats Prentiss' division. They surrendered before sundown, the whole kit and kiboodle. By now youll find them marching down the Corinth road, under a rebel guard."

So that was that. There was no use beating around the wet woods any longer, looking for an outfit ten miles away on the opposite side of the lines by now.

It sort of took the wind out of me, knowing that now I had no chance to get back to the ones I'd walked away from, no chance to make it up to them the way I'd planned. Then for a minute I had a crazy notion to go back to the big oak near the log house and report to Grant: "General, here's an unattached cannoneer, got his nerve back at last and wants a share in the fighting tomorrow morning."

It was just a notion; of course I'd never do a thing like that. But then I remembered the siege guns, the ones strung out along the ridge where the campfires were. I'd never served any piece larger than a twelve-pounder, but I thought I might be of some use swabbing the bore or carrying ammunition or something—this six-foot-five of mine always came in handy when heavy work was called for. So I went back the way I came, past the sleeping men and the log hospital where they were still hard at work (the amputation pile reached the window ledge now, beginning to spread out into the yard) and up to where the line of campfires began on the ridge. That was when I saw for the first time that all the cannons werent big ones. There were some light pieces mixed in, looking like toys alongside the siege guns.

I was making my way up to one of the light pieces, thinking maybe I could have my old job again— Number Four, back on the handspike—when I tripped over someone rolled in his blanket. My shoe must have hit him in the ribs, for he gave a grunt and a groan and raised himself on one elbow. Then firelight flickered on his face, showing his mouth all set to start cussing, and I could hardly believe my eyes. It was Lieutenant Pfaender.

I said, "Scuse me, lieutenant."

"Whynt you go where youre looking?" he mumbled, and rolled back over and went to sleep again. He was so tired he hadnt even recognized me, or else he'd forgot I'd ever been gone.

What had happened, they had got away from the sunken road just before the surrender, bringing off two guns, and when Lieutenant Pfaender reported to Colonel Webster back at the overlook, the colonel put what was left of the battery in line with the siege guns. Theyd had a share in breaking the final charge that came just before dark. I didnt know that now, though, and I was certainly surprised to find them here after being told they were surrendered.

I went on to the gun. The crew members, those that were left, together with some of the men from guns that had been lost, were sleeping on both sides of the trail. Sergeant Buterbaugh sat with his back against a caisson wheel, smoking his pipe upside-down because of the rain. Corporal Keller was asleep beside him; he had a bandage round his head. The sergeant watched me come up, then took the pipe out of his mouth.

"What happened to you?"

"I was scared," I said; "I ran. You want to make something *of* it?" That made me mad, having him ask a thing like that when he already knew the answer.

He put the pipe back in his mouth, puffing. "Go on, bed down," he said. "We've got a rough day coming up tomorrow."

5 *Sergeant Jefferson Polly Scout, Forrest's Cavalry*

Near midnight the storm broke over us. It had been raining since sundown, a steady drizzle with occasional gusts of wind to drive it, but now there was thunder, rolling and rumbling like an artillery fight, and great yellow flashes of lightning brighter than noonday. The wind rose, howling in the underbrush and whipping against our faces, even through the upturned collars of our captured overcoats, and by the flashes of lightning we saw the trees bent forward like keening women and trembling along their boughs. We made our way down a ravine, one of those deep gullies which were supposed to drain the tableland into the Tennessee but which were thigh-deep with backwater now, all of them, because of the rising river.

There were Indian mounds in the woods beyond the rim of the gully. Earlier in the day, soon after the surrender of Prentiss, I stood on the tallest of these, right at the bluff overlooking the Landing, and watched troops come ashore off the steamboats. When I'd been there long enough to make certain they were reinforcements from Buell's army finally marching in from Columbia, I went back the way I had come, located the colonel, and reported what I'd seen. He never had any reason to doubt anything I'd told him so far, but this was too big to pass on as hearsay, and as usual he wanted to see for himself.

He chose six troopers, dressed us all eight (including himself) in the blue Federal overcoats we had picked up in the captured camp that afternoon on the chance they might come in handy, and told me to strike out, guiding the way, and he would have a look-see. I was worried for fear I would lose the path because things were so different with the storm brewing, but I picked my way from stone to tree as I recognized them by lightning flashes, and at last came to the base of the mound. That was a relief, as you would know if youd ever seen Forrest with his dander up. There were about a dozen of these mounds in this corner of the tableland, put up by Indians in the olden days before the white men—I suppose for tribal purposes: burial, maybe. They varied in size from just little dirt-packs six or eight feet high, to real hills maybe thirty feet up in the air. Mine was the largest and not really hard to find; I had no real cause for all that worry. It stood out directly above the lower end of the bluff, overlooking the Landing.

Forrest told the others to stand guard at the base, and he and I began to climb the steep western face of the mound. This was easier said than done, for the rain had made it slippery. We had to hold onto each other and onto bushes and small trees, pulling ourselves up hand over hand, slipping and sliding in the mud and catching our spurs against creepers and blackberry bushes.

Just before we reached the top there was an explosion on the other side and a great flash of red outlining the mound. At first I thought one of the steamboats had blown her boiler, but then there was a sound of wind rushing *whoosh!* past our ears, and a long trail of sparks against the night. Almost immediately there came a second explosion, the same flash of red followed by another rush of wind: whoosh! and the paling arc of the fuze along the sky. Forrest had his face turned toward me when the second one went off. His chin beard was black against his face.

"Its the gunboats," I said. "We'll see them directly."

From the eastern slope we saw them anchored not

far from bank, near where a branch ran out of the gully and into the river. There were two of them and we were looking almost straight down onto their decks. The gunners had rolled back the big naval cannons; now they were busy swabbing them, getting ready for the next shots ten minutes later. Their shells had been falling out on the battlefield, among the wounded and sleeping Federals and Confederates, coming down on schedule ever since dusk-dark, two every fifteen minutes. They were so big and they made such a God-awful racket going off, the men called them lampposts and wash pots.

Not more than half a mile downstream and about a hundred feet below, we could see Buell's soldiers coming ashore. They came off the steamboats onto a wharf where torches were burning. All up and down the bank, in both directions from the Landing, the stretch of ground between the bluff and the river was crowded with men. Most of them were in shadow, dark splotches against the pale yellow sand, but when the lightning flashed—sometimes it lasted through time to count to five—we could see their faces, shrunk to the size of your palm across that distance and pale as magnolia petals. They were the ones who had left the fight, lost heart, thrown in their cards and skedaddled as soon as the going got rough. Part of my training was learning to look at bodies of troops and tell how many men were among them. I was never one to throw figures around carelessly anyhow. But I will say this, here and now: There were at least six thousand Yankee soldiers skulking under that bluff.

Not all of them were sitting on the bank. Some were out on the wharf, trying to squeeze past the incoming men to find a place on the steamboats. Others were waist-deep in the water, trying to climb the sides of the boats, but there were sailors stationed along the gangways to keep them off by banging their fingers and heads with marlin spikes and belaying pins. We could hear the sailors cussing them, and whenever there was a lull in the roar that came up from the riverbank, we heard the men in the water offering money and gratitude if theyd let them aboard. It was the kind of thing that would make a man ashamed to be part of their army. If it hadnt been for having seen blue-bellies as brave as any men I ever knew out on the battlefield that afternoon—in the Hornets Nest, along that sunken road—I'd have said the war couldnt last another week, not with men like those wearing the uniform. I felt almost ashamed for them, because after all it was once our country too.

Boats moved back and forth across the river, their wheels beating a white, foamy wake in the black water and drops shining like diamonds as they dripped from the paddles in the torchlight beside the wharf. Men came off the boats six deep, shouldering their way through the skulkers and marching up the bluff road to the tableland above, joining the line of battle where the fighting stopped at dark.

"There they are," I said: "Buell's men come on from Columbia. More than we've got left after the all-day fight, and ready to hit us first thing in the morning."

We watched them come off, regiment after regiment, as fast as the boats could make it down to Savannah for a fresh load. Forrest didnt say anything. Crouched in the mud, looking down on them, he didnt need to say anything for me to know what he was thinking, because having been with him for nine months now I could the same as hear him thinking out loud. He knew something had to be done before daylight. We had to hit them in a night attack, by coming up the way I'd brought him, or get off that tableland before they charged us in the morning.

When Beauregard called off the fight at sundown he had every reason to think the next day would be spent picking up the spoils of battle. He had Grant's army pushed back within shooting distance of the river and he had received a dispatch telling him that Buell's army had reversed its route of march and was moving toward Decatur. But now Forrest had seen with his own eyes how wrong the dispatch was. For a quarter of an hour we watched the reinforcements coming ashore, the thick blue columns marching up the bluff. Then the gunboats fired again, both shells screaming past with their breath in our hair. Forrest got up, still without saying anything, and went back down the mound.

The six troopers were there (they gave me a start for a moment, wearing those dark overcoats, until I remembered I was wearing one too) but he didnt even stop to tell them what he'd seen. I knew where he was headed. The nearest troops were Chalmers' brigade, camped on the ground where Prentiss had surrendered before sundown. Forrest was going to Chalmers, tell him what he'd seen, and persuade him to use his brigade in a night attack on the Landing or at least bring them down the ravine to a position from which they could fire into the stragglers and the reinforcements coming in. Or if it was too late for that— which it well might be—he was going to Beauregard, wherever *he* was, and tell him it was a question of clear out or be whipped.

When the battle opened Sunday morning, we were posted with the 1st Tennessee Infantry on the south side of Lick Creek, guarding the fords. From sunup until almost noon we stayed there, hearing the guns roaring and the men cheering as they charged through camp after camp. About midmorning the infantry crossed over, marching toward the firing, but we stayed there under orders, patrolling the creek with no sign of a bluecoat in sight and the battle racket getting fainter. Finally the colonel had enough of that. So he assembled the regiment and gave us a speech. (Forrest enjoyed putting on a little show every now and again, conditions permitting.) He stood in the stirrups and addressed us.

"Boys, you hear that musketry and that artillery?"

"Yair! Yair!" It came in a roar.

"Do you know what it means?" But he wasnt asking; he was telling us. "It means our friends are falling by hundreds at the hands of the enemy. And here we are, guarding a damned crick! We didnt enter the service for such work while we're needed elsewhere. Lets go help them! What do you say?"

It came in a roar: "Yair! Yair!"

So he led the way across the creek and we followed, splashing. There was a litter of canteens and haversacks and discarded rifles—this ground had already been taken. The wounded looked up with fever-hot eyes, Union and Confederate, from back in the bushes where they had crawled to be out of the way. After we'd ridden about a mile, looking for a place where we could do some good, Forrest put us in line on a road in rear of Cheatham's division, which had just been thrown back from an attack. The infantry lay on the grass, blown and surly because their charge had failed.

While we were lined up there, waiting to support the infantry when they went forward again, the artillery opened on us. This was not as bad as you might think, for at that range, by careful watching, we could see the balls coming and clear a path for them. It was no fun, however. When they had given us a couple of salvos and were coming in on the range, Forrest rode over to General. Cheatham, who was sitting his horse with his staff about him. It had begun to get hot, the sun high and bright as hammered gold. Forrest was in his shirtsleeves, his coat folded across the pommel of his saddle. He saluted and Cheatham returned it.

"General, I cant let my men stay here under this fire. I must either move forward or fall back."

Cheatham looked at him—we were no part of his command and I suppose he figured he had enough to look after already. "I cannot give you the order," he said. "If you make the charge it will be under your own orders."

"Then I'll do it," Forrest said. "I'll charge under my own orders."

And with that he came jingling back to where we were dodging cannonballs, wheeling our horses with the intent precision of men dancing a mounted minuet. The colonel's color had risen, the way it always did in a fight. His eyes had that battle-glint in them already.

Beyond the road where the infantry had formed there was a field skirted with timber along its flanks and rear—blackjack mostly, thick with underbrush— and in the opposite far corner there was a peach orchard in full bloom, the blossoms like pink icing on a cake. Here were two Federal batteries and a heavy line of troops lying beneath the peach trees, firing. Smoke lazed and swirled up through the bright pink blossoms. Another battery was in position to the left of the orchard, across the field and at the edge of the timber. When they saw we were forming for attack, the gunners changed direction and began to range in on us.

Before they found the range we rode forward, advancing four deep on a wide front. When the battery pulled its shots in, sending them close again, Forrest signaled the bugler and we changed front, moving by the left flank into fours. The gunners shifted their pieces. But by the time they had us lined up (they were green) the bugle blared again and we came back on a regimental front. The horses were beginning to snort now, hoofs drumming on the turf. It was pretty, I tell you, and we were feeling mighty proud of ourselves. But next time they were too quick for us. As we came back into fours a ball took out the file behind me, killing two troopers and all four of the horses. We heard their bones crunch—blood spattered fifteen or twenty yards in both directions. By this time we had zigzagged to within rushing distance of the battery. When we came about by the right flank, back on a wide front once more, the bugle sounded the charge. We went forward at a gallop, sabers out.

Forrest was in front. He stood in the stirrups, taller than life in his shirtsleeves, swinging that long razor-sharp saber—anyone within reach got cut; blue or gray, it didnt matter—and bellering "Charge! Charge!" in a voice that rang like brass.

The guns gave us a volley of grape, but when we came through the smoke I saw cannoneers breaking for the blackjack thickets where it was too dense for us to follow on horses. Then I saw for the first time that the infantry had come on behind. Cheatham's men whooped and hollered round the guns.

We drew back and formed our ranks again. The colonel was beginning to fret because he couldnt find anyone with authority to tell him where he was wanted. I suppose, too, he was feeling a bit guilty about leaving the Lick Creek fords unguarded. He told Lieutenant Strange, the adjutant, to report to

General Beauregard for orders. Strange was a top-notch soldier when it came to paper work (he was regimental sergeant major until the reorganization two weeks before) but Forrest wasnt so sure how well he would do when it came to finding his way around on the battlefield, so he told me to go along with him.

We rode toward the left, following what had been the line of battle an hour or two before. There was worse confusion on this part of the field than any we had seen since we crossed the creek. The wounded were thicker and the captured camps were crowded with men who had stopped to plunder. Passing a Yankee general's tent I saw four Confederate privates sitting in a ring around a keg of whiskey. They were drunk already, passing a gourd from hand to hand and wiping their mouths with their cuffs. Off to one side, demonstrating the privilege of rank, a big sandy-haired corporal sat with a demijohn all to himself. At another place, a little farther along, the woods had caught fire. Most of the wounded had crawled clear, or had been dragged out by friends, but I heard others squalling beyond the flames.

No one knew where Beauregard's headquarters was, until we lucked up on Colonel Jordan, his chief of staff, who told us we would find the general at Shiloh Meeting House, a log cabin over toward the

left, on the Corinth road. We went the way he said
and there it was. I waited at the road-fork with the
horses while Strange went in to report.

While I was standing there, holding the reins of
both horses, a tow-headed boy wearing a homespun
shirt under his jacket came up to me. He was about
seventeen, just beginning to raise some fuzz on his
cheeks. He carried his left arm across his stomach,
holding it by the wrist with the other hand. The
sleeve of the hurt arm was caked with blood from
just below the shoulder all the way down to the cuff.

"Whar's a doctor?" he said, his voice trembling.

I told him I didnt know but there should be some of
them over toward the right, where the sound of the
fighting had swelled up again, and he went on. He
was sad to see: had a dazed look around the eyes, as
if he'd seen things no boy ought to see, and he
wobbled as he walked. I thought to myself: Boy,
you better lie down while you can.

Finally Strange came out of the meeting house and
we turned back the way we had come. That seemed
the sensible thing to do, though Lord knows there
was no telling where the regiment was by now.
They might be almost anywhere on the whole wide
battlefield, with Forrest leading them.

Strange said he hadnt talked to old Bory himself
but one of the aides had told him there was nothing

unusual about not knowing where to go for orders. The battle was being fought that way, he said—It was just a matter of helping whoever needed help most at the time. That seemed to me to be a mighty loose-jointed way to fight a war.

When we got past the place where we left Forrest the sun was near the landline. There was a great yelling in the woods beyond, and just as we rode up we met what I thought was the whole Yank army coming toward us. Then I saw they were marching without rifles or colors and they were under guard. It was what was left of Prentiss' division, surrendered when the other Union outfits fell back, leaving them stranded, and our regiment and most of Chalmers' brigade got between them and the river. They looked glum as glum but they had no cause for shame. They were the fightingest men in the whole blue-belly army, bar none, and if they hadnt held that sunken road in the Hornets Nest for six hours, it would have been all up with Grant before sundown.

Beyond the woods, in the little clearing where Prentiss had surrendered, our troopers and the men of Chalmers' Mississippi brigade were trying to out-yell each other. Their lips were black from the cartridge bite and their voices came shrill across the field while the sun went down on the other side of the battleground, big and red through the trees. The colonel was still in his shirtsleeves, sitting with one leg across the pommel, smiling and watching the fun. When Strange told him what Beauregard's aide had said, I suppose he was easier in his mind—knowing he'd done right—but then again maybe I'm wrong; maybe it hadnt bothered him at all. Forrest was never one to let orders keep him from doing what he knew was best.

That was when I left to go out and do some scouting on my own. The regiment went on to support Chalmers and Jackson in their attacks against the siege guns drawn in a half-circle along the ridge near the bluff. They charged those guns, up the ridge, until Beauregard sent word to call it a day. But I had no part in that. Following the ravine down toward the river in the gathering dusk, I came upon the Indian mound, climbed it, and lay there for nearly an hour, counting troops and hearing them identify themselves as they came ashore.

They were really obliging about that. Every now and then, when the steamboat neared bank, some rambunctious Fed would lean over the rail and yell at the skulkers: "Never mind, boys. Here's the 6th Indiana, come to win your damned battle for you!" It was Buell's Army of the Ohio—no doubt about that: I identified them regiment after regiment coming ashore. Some of the outfits were ones we'd badgered during our operation along the Green River, back in January.

By the time I knew all I needed, it was full dark and had begun to rain, first a fine mist like spray, then a slow steady drizzle coming down through the branches with a quiet murmuring sound against the blackberry bushes. I went back. It was no easy job in the dark. Being in a hurry, I stumbled and slipped in the mud—I must have fallen at least a dozen times, getting disoriented every time. And to cap the climax, as if I wasnt mad enough already, when I got back I couldnt locate the colonel.

I found the camp, all right: just blundered into it. But Forrest was out in the field somewhere, they told me, looking for Willy, his fifteen-year-old son, who had struck out with two other boys that afternoon on a little operation of their own. Long past dark, when they still had not come back, the colonel went out looking for them. Mrs Forrest (she was the only person the colonel was really afraid of) had specially charged him to look out for Willy from the day she let Forrest take him with him to enlist.

That was in Memphis, June of '61, a month before his fortieth birthday. He went down to the recruiting office and signed up as a private in a horse company, taking his youngest brother and his son. He had voted against secession but when Tennessee left the Union he left with her. By the time of Shiloh he had already made a name for himself: first by bringing his command out of Donelson after the generals decided to surrender, then by taking charge at Nashville and saving the government stores during the hubbub that followed General Johnston's retreat—but most of the talk was wild. Because he didnt speak the way they did in their parlors, or fight the way it showed in their manuals, they said he was an illiterate cracker who came barefoot out of the hills in overalls and right away began to show his genius. They meant it well; it made good listening. But it was just not true.

Bedford Forrest was born in Middle Tennessee, son of a blacksmith and a pioneer woman named Beck. When he was sixteen his father died and left him head of a family of nine in the backwoods section of North Mississippi where they had moved three years before. He grew up there, working for an uncle in a livery stable. By the time he was twenty-four he was a partner and had met the girl he intended to marry. Her guardian was a Presbyterian minister, and when Forrest went to ask for her hand the old man turned him down:

"Why, Bedford, I couldnt consent. You cuss and gamble, and Mary Ann is a Christian girl."

"I know it," Forrest said. "Thats why I want her."

And he got her, too. The old man officiated at the wedding.

He got most things he went after. Within six years he had outgrown the Mississippi hamlet and moved to Memphis, expanding his livestock trade to include real estate and slaves. Ten years later, when the war began, he was worth beyond a million dollars and owned five thousand acres of plantation land down in the Delta. What the citizens of Memphis thought of him is shown by the fact that they elected him to the Board of Aldermen three times straight running. So when people say Forrest came into the war barefoot and in overalls, they arent telling the truth; theyre spreading the legend.

Less than a month after he enlisted he was called back to Memphis by Governor Harris and given authority to recruit a cavalry battalion of his own. That was the real beginning of his military career, and that was the first time I saw him.

I was on my way to Richmond, just passing through from Galveston, when I saw the notice in the *Appeal*:

I desire to enlist five hundred able-bodied men, mounted and equipped with such arms as they can procure (shot-guns and pistols preferable) suitable to the service. Those who cannot entirely equip themselves will be furnished arms by the State.

146

And I thought: Well, as well here as there. It had the sound of a man I could work for. I had reached that stage in my life where it didnt matter which way the cat jumped, and besides, I was tired of riding the train. It was mid-July of the hottest summer I ever knew. Cigar smoke writhed in long gray tendrils about the hotel room; the air was like a breath against my face. Sitting there beside the high window with the newspaper folded in my lap, I knew I had ended a six-year chase after nothing.

My father was a Baptist preacher in Houston. He'd come to Texas from Georgia (on the call of the Lord, he said) and when he had founded his church and was a pillar of society, he channeled all the drive that had brought him West into making me all he'd hoped to be. I never felt he was doing it for me, though: I always felt he was doing it for himself. He thought he was doing fine, too, until the day he got the letter from the head of the divinity school in Baltimore telling him I'd been dismissed for immorality, and all his dreams went bang. I was never cut out to be a preacher anyhow. When the proctor came into the room that Saturday night and stood there with his eyes bugged out, looking at the whiskey bottles and the girl my roommate and I had picked up on the waterfront, I was almost glad. It meant an end to trying to be something I was never meant to be. I packed and left.

All I knew about making my way in the world was what I'd learned from a thousand divinity tracts and a half-hour lecture my father once gave me on the benefits of purity. I sold my clothes and shipped as a seaman on a British bark bound round the Cape with a cargo of hemp for the California coast. I was nineteen at the time and I had never hit a lick of work in my life.

I jumped ship in Los Angeles, got a berth as driver with a wagon train heading east for Missouri, and left them in Kansas to join another one rolling west. It was like that for six years—I tried everything I could imagine. I was faro dealer in a Monterey gambling hell, wore a tall silk hat and a claw-hammer coat with a derringer up one sleeve; but I couldnt make the cards behave, so they dealt me out. In Utah I sold buffalo meat to Mormons. I panned for gold on the Sacramento River and was a harvest hand in Minnesota. I worked as a bouncer in a San Francisco saloon but got bounced so often myself they let me go. I was a mule skinner with a pack train out of Denver and nearly died of thirst after running into trouble with Apaches in the Colorado Desert. Six years was enough: I shipped round the Cape again, this time on a Massachusetts schooner, and docked at Galveston in late June of '61. I'd intended to go up to Houston then, to see if my father was alive; but when I heard there was a war on, I put it out of my mind completely, the way you close a book.

For some men war meant widows' tears and orphans' howls. For me it meant another delay before time to go to my father and admit I'd done as poor a job of making a bad man as I had of making a good one. I decided to go to Richmond to see the lay of the land, then to Wilmington or maybe Charleston to join the Confederate navy. I preferred fighting on water; it seemed cleaner. But when I stopped over-night in Memphis, between trains, and saw the notice in the paper, I changed my mind and settled for the cavalry under Forrest.

The recruiting office was in the Gayoso House— the colonel's brother Jeffrey swore me in. While I was waiting for there to be enough of us to go in a group to our quarters upstairs, Forrest entered from Main Street. He was tall, over six feet, narrow in the hips and broad-shouldered, with the flat legs of a natural horseman. His hair was iron gray, worn long and brushed back on both sides of a rounded widow's peak above a high forehead. Between a wide mus-tache and a black chin-beard his lips were full but firm. His nose was straight, nostrils flared, and his eyes were gray-blue. They looked directly at you when he spoke (I never saw such eyes before or since) and his voice was low, though later I was to hear it rise to a brassy clangor that sounded from end to end of the line, above the sound of guns and hoofs.

From that first instant when I saw him walk into the lobby of the Gayoso, I knew I was looking at the most man in the world. Afterwards—in Kentucky rounding up horses and men and equipment, then back in camp at the Memphis Fair Grounds, then fighting gunboats on the Cumberland when no one believed they could be fought, then in the attack at Sacramento when I first saw him stand in the stirrups and beller "Charge!" and then out of the wreck of Donelson across freezing creeks and back-water saddle-skirt deep—I followed him and watched him grow to be what he had become by the time of Shiloh: the first cavalryman of his time, one of the great ones of *all* time, though no one realized it that soon except men who had fought under him.

I was a scout by then, operating out beyond the rim of the army and dropping back from time to time to report. I liked that work. Sometimes it took me far from headquarters, beyond the Union lines. Sometimes it was simpler. At Shiloh it was much simpler. I went to the Indian mound, saw Buell's men coming ashore, and came back to tell Forrest what I'd seen. The only trouble was I couldnt find him.

There was no use floundering around on the battle-field looking for him while he was looking for Willy, so I waited at headquarters. It was a long wait, sitting there while rain drummed on the captured tent fly. Then, about eleven oclock—not long before the weather broke in earnest—the colonel and his son arrived from opposite directions. Willy was his special concern, not only because he was likely to get his head blown off poking it into every corner of the fighting, but also because the boy had begun to pick up soldier talk and soldier manners, and Mrs Forrest had warned her husband to look out for his deportment as well as his safety. A week before, while we were at Monterey, the colonel rode over to Polk's camp, borrowed the sons of Bishop Otey and General Donelson (they were about Willy's age, fifteen) and brought them back so Willy would have someone his own age to be with.

Forrest returned first. He was dripping wet, angry, and worried. I usually steered clear of him at such times but this couldnt wait. Just as I was about to report, however, there was a whoop of laughter and catcalls, and through the opening of the tent we saw the three boys marching a batch of prisoners in the rain. They had struck out together soon after the taking of the Peach Orchard, making a tour of the field, and on the way back they came upon a group of about a dozen Yank stragglers in a ravine near the river—a sorry, bedraggled lot sitting like mudturtles on some logs. The boys threw down on them with their shotguns, put them in column, and marched them into camp. Reporting to the colonel with their prisoners, they were the three proudest boys in the Confederacy. Forrest was so pleased and amused he even forgot to scold them.

But he became serious enough when I told him what I'd seen from the overlook. He called for the six troopers and we put on the blue overcoats and went out. As soon as he had found out for himself that what I reported was true, we came back down the mound and he led the way straight for the camp of Chalmers, whose troops were sleeping on the ground where Prentiss surrendered. The general was asleep when we got there, but Forrest made one of the aides wake him up. He came out to us still in his fighting clothes, a young man, his eyes puffed almost shut with fatigue and his hair rumpled in a wave on one side from sleeping on it.

His troops had done some of the hardest fighting on the field, and when he bedded them down for the night he didnt doubt that tomorrow would complete the victory. Hearing that the Army of the Ohio had come up, he shook his head—he couldnt believe it. When Forrest made it clear that he himself had seen them arriving on steamboats from down the river, it jarred him completely awake. But he wouldnt agree to a night attack. His men were too weary, he said. Besides, he couldnt make an attack without orders from Corps or Army headquarters. Johnston was dead; he didnt know where to find either Bragg or Beauregard. So that was that as far as he was concerned. All through the scene Forrest's face had been getting redder and redder, a sure sign his anger was rising—I have seen his face go red as brickdust —and at last he stood up from the camp stool and shook his finger in General Chalmers' face.

"If the enemy comes on us in the morning, we'll be whipped like hell," he said. And stomped out.

It was the same everywhere we went. No brigadier was willing to make an attack without orders from above, not even those who realized that waiting for the Federals to complete their reinforcement meant sure defeat for us after daylight. The main difference between Chalmers and the other brigadiers we managed to stumble on was that he knew where his men were bivouacked—most of them had no idea. They were waiting for morning, they said, when they could get their troops into line and renew the attack. And every time they said this, Forrest got a little redder in the face and began to tremble and told them the same thing he'd told Chalmers: "We'll be whipped like hell." Then we'd go on to another camp, trying to persuade another general. Everywhere, always, it was the same—no attack without orders: the men were too tired to advance till they had their sleep out. Over and over again we heard it. It was enough to make an angel cuss, let alone N. B. Forrest.

I left him about one o'clock, dead on my feet, but he kept right on going from camp to camp, blundering around in the wet and the dark, trying to locate someone with enough rank and gumption to move against the landing. He finally found General Brackinridge, who was a corps commander—not to mention Vice President of the United States, just over a year ago, when we were all one country—but Breckinridge said that as head of the Army reserve he did not have the authority to order an attack. He didn't know where Beauregard was sleeping—nor Polk, he said, nor Bragg—but he told him where to find Hardee, and Hardee was a fighter.

But there it was even worse. Forrest couldnt so much as get past the staff, though at length he managed to see the AAG, a tall thin middle-aged man with a lisp, wearing a bathrobe and carpet slippers, who heard what Forrest had to say and then dismissed him, saying the information was sure to be known at

154

headquarters already. He yawned as he spoke, the words sounding hollow:

"You can rest assured they know whats best up there. We have already received orders to attack at day dawn." He tapped his teeth with his fingertips, yawning. "So go back to your troops, colonel, and keep up a strong and vigilant picket line all along your front."

This was the brand of talk that made Forrest maddest. Nine times out of ten he'd have exploded right there in the staff officer's face, would have reached out and grabbed him, bathrobe and all, but I suppose he knew it was too late already, even if he could have got Hardee to order an advance. Buell's army was mostly ashore by now, probably, and our men needed all the rest they could get for the fight against fresh troops tomorrow morning.

I took one of the blankets off the Yankee colonel's bed (—it would be Forrest's bed tonight; there was enough cover on it to wrap a regiment) and spread it on the ground in one corner of the tent. But before I even had time to tuck it round me I fell asleep. I knew I was tired but I hadnt known *how* tired. The minute my head came level with my feet, every muscle in my body turned to jelly. I took a deep breath, intending to heave a sigh, but I dont know to this good day whether I did or not. Before I could let it out again I was gone from this world, gone to what my old nurse back in Texas used to call Snooze land.

Next thing I knew, there was a thumping and groaning, mixed with a jingling and the sound of someone cussing a blue streak. I raised myself on one elbow, pulled the blanket around me at last, and looked across the tent. It was Forrest, sitting on the edge of the Yankee colonel's bed and wrastling his boots off. The jingling was the spurs, but the rest of it was just Forrest being angry. He was talking to himself, muttering something about a vigilant picket line, a bathrobe and a pair of carpet slippers. None of it made any sense to me. The lightning had stopped and so had the thunder. The wind had fallen, too, but the rain drummed steadily against the tent.

Just as I was about to get up and help him, tired as I was, he got the boots off and lay back on the bed, still mumbling. I could smell him; any time he got thoroughly mad you could smell it. Suddenly the tent was filled with snoring. I began to drift back to sleep myself, smelling the strong sweat of Forrest's anger and thinking how much I had lived through today and how different tonight was from last night, when we'd bivouacked on the south bank of Lick Creek and lain there listening to the Federal bands serenading us unbeknownst. For a second there flicked across my mind a picture of the boy who had come up to me that afternoon at the crossroads near the chapel and asked where a doctor was. I wondered if he made it—but only for a second: there were lots like him, and besides I was asleep by then.

The sound of firing woke me. Dawn had come, paling the canvas so that the first thing I saw when I opened my eyes was the big **U S** stenciled on the ceiling (I saw it in reverse: **S U**, directly above my head) and when I looked around I saw I was alone in the tent. When Forrest let a man sleep like that, it meant he was pleased with his work.

By the time I got myself unwrapped from the blanket and out in front of the tent, the firing had swelled to a steady clatter like the sound of a wagon crossing a canefield, stalks popping against the axle-tree. The Union infantry was roaring to the attack. Charging, they made a different sound from us. Ours was a high yipping series of yells, like foxhunters coursing, but theirs was a deep roar, like surf on a stormy night. It was somehow more organized, more concerted, as if they had practiced beforehand, and it came from down deep in their chests instead of up high in their throats.

They will tell you Shiloh was no cavalry battle; the field was too cut-up with ravines and choked with timber for the usual mounted work. However, none of Forrest's men realized this at the time, and we had our moments. By that time he'd developed us to the point where we were more horse-infantry than cavalry. We used our horses more to get there on than to fight on. That was his tactics: "Get there first with the most men"—only he didnt call it Tactics; he called it Bulge: "Fifteen minutes of bulge is worth a week of tactics," and his orders to us were always direct, in language a man could understand: "Shoot at everything blue and keep up the scare" or "Hit them on the end," where a West Pointer would have said: "Be aggressive" or "Engage them on the flank."

All through the long day's fight, while the battle went against us, we were not downhearted and we never failed to do whatever was required of us as long as the colonel was out front in his shirtsleeves, swinging that terrible sword. That was his way. He'd tried the night before to get them to do what he knew was right, and if the generals hadnt seen it his way he wasnt going to sit and sulk about it. We fought them mounted; we fought them dismounted, standing or running, all over that blasted field where the dead lay thick as leaves at harvest time. There was never a let-up until the thing was done.

Look at this notice he put in the Memphis *Appeal*;

he was up there recovering from his Fallen Timbers wound:

200 RECRUITS WANTED!

I will receive 200 able-bodied men if they will present themselves at my headquarters by the first of June with good horse and gun. I wish none but those who desire to be actively engaged.—Come on, boys, if you want a heap of fun and to kill some Yankees.

N. B. FORREST
Colonel, Commanding
Forrest's Regiment.

6 *Squad*
23d Indiana

I used to think how strange it was that the twelve of us had been brought together by an event which separated brothers and divided the nation. Each of us had his history and each of the histories was filled with accidental happenings.

Myself for instance: I was born in New England and was taken to Indiana, adopted me out of an orphanage. I was six at the time—I can barely remember. "Your name is Robert," they said; "Robert Winter." It was my first ride on a train. "You are our son Robert. We are taking you home." Then we ate sandwiches out of a paper bag. For years I thought all children came from Boston.

Thats what I mean by accidental. I had to be adopted out of a New England orphanage to become part of an Indiana squad. And it was the same all down the line. Every one of the twelve had his own particular story.

This tied in with what Corporal Blake said during one of the halts Sunday while we were marching from Stony Lonesome toward the sound of guns across the creek. He said books about war were written to be read by God Amighty, because no one but God ever saw it that way. A book about war, to be read by men, ought to tell what each of the twelve of us saw in our own little corner. Then it would be the way it was—not to God but to us.

I saw what he meant but it was useless talking. Nobody would do it that way. It would be too jumbled. People when they read, and people when they write, want to be looking out of that big Eye in the sky, playing God.

But the strange thing was that I should think of it now, lying before sunup on the edge of the battle-field. Then again, tired and wrought-up as we were from all the waiting and the bungled march the day before, I suppose almost anything could have come into my mind. We had marched onto the field after dark. The first I saw of it was when daylight filtered through and we were lying there waiting for the shooting to get started again. We werent green—we had seen our share of killing: but this was different to begin with. We had heard so many tales the night before. The army had been wrecked, they told us; we were marching in for the surrender.

Our division, Lew Wallace commanding, was in position on the east side of a hollow. There were woods thick on both sides and a creek down in the draw. Across it, half a mile away, where the opposite slope rose up in a bluff, the rebels were lined up waiting. We could see their battle flags and sunlight sparkling on a battery near the center of their line.

We were the flank division of Grant's army. Snake Creek, which we crossed the night before, was off to our right. When dawn broke and the sun came through the haze, I lay there in the grass, watching it glint on the fieldpieces, and I thought: Oh-oh. If Wallace sends us across that hollow in the face of those guns, he's going to have considerably fewer of us when we reach the other side.

There was a long quiet period, nearly an hour, while the two armies lay and looked across the vacant space like two dogs sizing each other up. Then firing began to sputter over on the left, like growling, nothing much at first but finally a steady clatter, growing louder and louder, swelling along the front toward where we lay.

"Hey, sarge," Winter said. "If they marched up here *look*ing for a fight, why dont they come on?"

I didnt answer. Then Klein: "Maybe they know Buell got in last night." Klein was always ready with some kind of remark.

"Let the generals plan the war," I told him. "All you are paid to do is fight it."

I really thought our time had come. But Wallace had more sense than to send us naked across that draw against those guns. He ordered up two of his batteries, one in front of where we were and another down the line. They tuned up, ranging in on the brassy glints on the bluff. We enjoyed watching them work. Thompson's battery, which was directly to our front, did especially well. We watched the balls rise like black dots, getting smaller, then come down on the rebel guns across the hollow. The cannoneers were lively, proud to be putting on a show, and every now and then we cheered them. It didnt last long. As soon as one of the secesh guns was dismounted by a direct hit, the whole battery limbered and got out. That was what we had been waiting for.

It's not often you see war the way a civilian thinks it is, but it was that way now. We were center brigade, and since our company—G—was just to the right of the brigade center, we saw the whole show. Wallace was directly in our rear, standing beside his horse and watching the artillery duel through his field glasses. Grant rode up with Rawlins and dismounted within six feet of Wallace, but Wallace was so busy with his glasses that he didnt know Grant was there until one of the division staff officers coughed nervously: "General . . ." Then Wallace turned and saw Grant.

There was bad blood between them and our poor showing yesterday hadnt helped matters. Wallace saluted and Grant returned it, touching the brim of his hat with the tips of his fingers. He had the look of a man who has missed his sleep. His uniform was rumpled even worse than usual, and he stood so as to keep the weight off his left ankle, which he had sprained two days ago when his horse fell on him.

I could not hear what they were saying (both batteries were going full blast now) but I saw Grant motion with his arm as he talked and Wallace kept nodding his head in quick, positive jerks. It was clear that Grant was indicating the direction of attack—he pointed toward the bluff, stabbing the air—but it seemed foolish to me, seeing we had been given our orders already.

When the rebel battery fell back, their infantry went with it. Grant mounted, still talking and motioning with his arm. Wallace kept nodding—Yes, I

understand: Yes—and Grant rode away, Rawlins jogging beside him.

Wallace passed between us and Company F. He
went about a hundred yards out front, then turned
his horse and faced us. This must have been some sort
of signal to the brigade commanders, for all the battle
flags tilted forward at once and the whole division
stepped out, advancing with brigades in echelon and
not even being fired on. It was pretty as a picture.

Until we struck the scrub oaks halfway down the
slope we could see from flank to flank, blue flags
uncased, snapping in the breeze, and the rifles of the
skirmishers catching sunlight. Wallace sat on his horse,
waiting for us to come past. As we opened ranks and
flowed around him, we put our caps on the ends of
our gun barrels and gave him a cheer. He raised himself in the saddle and lifted his hat as we went by.
His mustache was black against his high-colored face
and his teeth showed white beneath it. He was
thirty-four, the youngest major general in the army.

We went on, tramping through underbrush, walking with our rifles held crossways to keep from
getting slapped in the face by limbs. As we crossed
the creek I saw the line again for a couple of hundred
yards both right and left, the yellow water splashing
calf-deep as the men passed over. Then we were
climbing. We went on up—the bluff was not as steep

as it had looked from across the draw; it wasnt really a bluff at all—then reached the flat where the rebel cannon lay wrecked. Its bronze tube had been thrown sidewise, with a big dent at the breech where the cannonball came down, and both wheels were canted inward toward the broken splinter-bar. Off to one side lay a pinch-faced cannoneer, as dead as dead could be. With his long front teeth and his pooched-out cheeks he looked a little like a chipmunk. The men stood gawking at him.

"All right," I told them. "All right. Let it go."

The ground was high and level here, without so many trees, and we could see toward the left where the supporting division was supposed to have kept up. That was Sherman. But there were no men out there, either Union or Confederate, so we got orders from Captain Tubbs to form a defensive line till the front was restored.

I got the squad organized. So far so good, I thought. But I was beginning to feel a little jumpy. It was too easy: a walk in the woods on a sunny Monday morning, with nothing to bother us but wet socks from crossing the creek. There were bound to be hard things coming.

Talk about lucky—I never knew what it was. Just when everything was going good and I had organized myself a nice grassy spot to take it easy while the outfit on our left came even with us, I looked up and: spat: a big fat raindrop hit me square in the eye. At first they were few and far between, dropping one by one, plumping against the dead leaves with a sound like a leaky tap, then faster and faster, pattering—a regular summer shower. It had been bad enough trying to sleep in it the night before, with our oilcloths left back at Stony Lonesome. Now we were going to have to fight in it as well. For a while it rained in sunshine (the devil beating his wife) but soon that passed too; there was only the gray rain falling slant-wise, shrouding the woods.

We waited and waited, hunched over our cartridge boxes trying to keep the rain out. Sergeant Bonner was next to me, still wearing that coon-dog look on his face. I never knew a man so eager, so conscious of his stripes.

"Rebel weather," I said—to be saying something.

He said, "I reckon they dont like it any better than we do, Klein. It wets their powder just as damp as ours."

Bonner was like that. Either he wouldnt answer you at all or he would say something to catch you up short. Holliday, on my other flank, grinned at me through the rain, winking and jerking his head toward the sergeant. Grissom was on the other side of Holliday; he kept the breech of his rifle under his coat and held the palm of his hand over the muzzle to keep out the rain. Diffenbuch was farther down the line, squatting with his collar hiked up, not paying any mind to anyone.

On the far side of the sergeant, Joyner began to yell: "Come on down, Raymond. More rain more rest." He always called the rain Raymond—I never knew why. Joyner was a card. Once at Donelson, where we nearly froze to death, he kept us warm just laughing at him, till his face went numb with the cold and he couldnt talk.

After a while the rain slacked up and Thompson's battery began to bang away at a column of johnnies coming along a road to the right. That started the trouble. Somewhere out beyond the curtain of steely rain—it was thinner now but we still couldnt see more than a couple of hundred yards in any direction —there began to be a series of muffled sounds, sort of like slapping a mattress with a stick, and right behind the booms came some whistling sounds arching toward us through the trees: artillery. We lay there, hugging the ground, never minding the wet. Every now and then one was low, bopping around and banging against the tree trunks. It was nothing new to us. But it was no fun either.

The rain stopped during the cannonade, almost as quick as it started, and the sun came out again. Everything glistened shiny new. We were at the edge of a big field. Beyond a strip of woods on the right was another field even bigger. In the trees at the other end of the far field, just as the sun came clear, we saw a host of grayback cavalry bearing down on the third brigade with their flashing sabers looking clean and rain-washed too. They rode through the skirmishers, on toward the main line. There they met a volley from massed rifles. It was as if they had run into a trip wire. Men and horses went down in a scramble, all confused, and the column turned, what was left of it, and rode back through the woods. It all happened in a hurry. Except for the wounded skirmishers, walking back with blood running down their faces from the saber hacks, they hadnt hurt us at all.

Lavery said, "Wasnt that pretty, Diff?"

I didnt see anything pretty about it, God forgive him.

Sherman finally caught up and we went forward together, across the first field, through the fringe of trees, and into the second, crossing toward where the cavalry charge had begun. When we were within a hundred yards, still holding our fire, a long deep line of men in gray jackets and brown wide-brim hats stood up from the brush and fired directly in our faces. It was the loudest noise I ever heard, and the brightest flash. There was artillery mixed up in it, too.

I fired one round, not even taking aim, and wheeled off at a run for the rear. Half the secret of being a good soldier is knowing when to stand and when to run—the trouble was, so many got killed before they learned it. But there was no doubt about which to do now.

We stopped in the woods between the two fields. Bonner began to count heads. Klein and Winter were missing. "All right," Bonner said. "Lets form! Lets form!"

Then Klein came walking up. That Klein: he'd stayed out with the skirmishers a while. He said, "I waited to give them a chance to shoot at you birds before I crawled back across that field. I'm nobody's fool."

"Lets form!" Sergeant Bonner was yelling. "Lets form!"

Before too long all three brigades were in line at

173

the fringe of trees between those two fields. The skirmishers—Nebraska boys—stayed out in the open, lying behind hillocks and brush clumps, firing into the woods where the rebels had stood up to blast us. When we went forward this time, passing the skirmishers, we knew what we would meet. That made a difference. Crossing, we stopped from time to time to fall on one knee, fire and reload, and worked our way ahead like that. Fifty yards short of the woods we gave them a final volley and went in with the bayonet. This time it was the johnnies ran.

We took some prisoners there, our first for the day. They were a scraggly lot. Their uniforms were like something out of a ragbag and they needed haircuts worse than any men I ever saw. They had beards of all kinds, done up to make them look ferocious, those that were old enough to grow them, and they had a way of talking—jabber jabber—that I couldnt follow. They were from Louisiana, Frenchies off the New Orleans wharfs. They called themselves the Crescent Regiment and were supposed to be one of the best the Confederates had on the field. They didnt look so capable to me.

That was the first hard fighting of the day. We ran into plenty just like it and some more that was worse, but generally speaking it was nothing like as bad as we expected. To hear the stragglers tell it

174

when we came across Snake Creek the previous night, we were going to be cut to pieces before sunup. It turned out there was plenty of cutting done, but we were the ones who did it, not the rebels. Maybe they were fought to a frazzle the day before, or maybe the news that Buell had come up took the wind out of their sails, or maybe they had already decided to retreat. Anyhow, every time we really pushed them they gave.

So if Wallace was worried about his reputation because of our poor showing on the Sunday march, he could stop fretting now. We more than redeemed ourselves in the Monday fight.

This goes back. Sunday morning we'd waked up hearing firing from the direction of Pittsburg, five miles south. It began like a picket clash but it grew to a regular roar, the heavy booming of cannon coming dull behind the rattle of musketry. It may have been our imagination but we thought we felt the ground tremble. The three brigades of our division were strung out two miles apart on the road running west —the first at Crump's Landing on the Tennessee, the second (ours) at Stony Lonesome, and the third at Adamsville, a little over four miles from Crump's.

Soon after the sound of battle grew heavy we got orders to send our baggage to the Landing for safe keeping. The other brigades marched in from east and west, joining us at our camp. Wallace didnt know whether he was going to have to defend his present position or be prepared to march to the table-land back of Pittsburg. In either case he had to concentrate and Stony Lonesome was the place for that. If there was an attack here, it was best not to receive it with our backs too close to the river. If we were to march to Pittsburg to reinforce Grant's other divisions, there were two roads we could take. They ran from our camp like a V, both crossing Snake Creek on the right flank of the army.

I went to Crump's as corporal in charge of the baggage detail. When I got there I saw Grant's dispatch steamer, the *Tigress*, putting in for bank. Grant was standing on the texas deck. He had pulled his hat down over his eyes, against the morning sun, and his hands were on the railing. Wallace waited on another steamer tied at the wharf. Grant's headquarters were at Savannah in a big brick house overlooking the river; every morning he made the nine-mile trip to Pittsburg to inspect the training. The way they told it later, he had just sat down to the breakfast table this Sunday morning and was lifting his coffee cup when he heard cannons booming from up the river. He put down the cup without taking a sip, went straight to the wharf, boarded the *Tigress*, and ordered the captain to make full steam for Pittsburg.

Passing Crump's, the pilot warped in and Grant leaned over the rail and yelled to Wallace: "General, get your troops under arms and have them ready to move at a moment's notice." Wallace shouted back that he'd already done this. Grant nodded approval and the pilot brought the *Tigress* about in a wide swing (she hadnt even slowed) and took her up the river.

That was about eight oclock. When I got back to Stony Lonesome all three brigades were there, the troops resting by the side of the road with their packs on the grass and their rifles across their knees. The colonels, expecting march orders any minute, hadnt even allowed them to stack arms. I reported to the first sergeant and he sent me back to the squad.

Sergeant Bonner was arguing with Klein about whether Klein could take his pack off. All the other squads had shed theirs long ago, and Klein was telling him he was torturing his men just to impress the officers; he was stripe-struck, Klein said, working for a dome on his chevrons. Bonner was riled—which was what Klein wanted—and just bull-headed enough to make us keep them on, now that Klein had made an issue of it. But finally he saw it was no use. "All right," he said. "Drop them." He didnt look at Klein as he said it. Klein took his pack off and leaned back smiling.

Youd think twelve men who had been through as much as we had (and who expected to go through even worse, perhaps, within a very short time) would make it a point to get along among themselves. Most of us hated the army anyhow, shoved as we were away down here in this Rebel wilderness. Youd think we would try to make up for it by finding some sort of enjoyment in our squad relationships. But no. Not a waking hour passed that one of us wasnt bickering, nursing a grudge. I blamed it all on Bonner at one time; morale was one of his responsibilities. Then I saw it wouldnt be a lot different under anyone else. We hated the army; we hated the war (except when we were actually fighting it; *then* you dont have time)—and we took it out on each other.

We lounged there beside the road, chewing grass stems and sweating. The sun rose higher. From time to time the sound of guns would swell and then die down. Occasionally they faded to almost nothing, a mutter, and we would think perhaps it was over; Grant had surrendered. But then it would come up louder than ever. Some said the sound moved toward the left, which would mean Grant was retreating; others said it moved toward the right, which would mean he was advancing. Myself, I couldnt tell. Sometimes it seemed to go one way, then another.

Wallace and his staff, orderlies holding their horses, were across the road from our company. That was about the center of the column, the point where the road branched off toward the fighting. Whenever the sound swelled louder, Wallace would raise his head and stare in that direction. He would take out his watch, look at it hard for a moment, then put it back in his pocket and shake his head, fretting under Grant's instructions to hold his troops in position till orders came. He didnt like it.

We stayed there three hours, and it seemed longer. At eleven-thirty a quartermaster captain galloped up on a lathered horse, dismounted, and handed Wallace a folded piece of paper. The general read it hurriedly, then slowly. He asked the captain something, and when the captain answered, Wallace turned to his staff. Within two minutes the couriers passed us on their horses, going fast.

At that time the cooks were passing out grub. It was beans as usual. The orders were, finish eating within half an hour, fall in on the road, and be prepared to march hard. By noon we were under way toward the sound of firing.

Then was when trouble began. From Stony Lonesome two roads ran south to the battlefield, both of them crossing Snake Creek, which was the right boundary. They formed a V with its angle at our starting point. The right arm of the V ran to a bridge connecting us with Sherman's line of camps. Wallace had had this bridge strengthened and the road corduroyed (I was on the detail myself, and a nasty detail it was, too) not only for an emergency such as this, in which Sherman needed us, but also for an emergency in which we would need Sherman—it worked both ways. So when Wallace got orders to join the right flank of Grant's army, he naturally took this road. But that was when trouble began, as I said.

It was five miles to the bridge. We were within a mile of it when a major from Grant's staff passed us with his horse in a lope. Shortly afterwards we were halted. It was hot and the dust was thick. We stood there. Soon we were surprised to see the head of the column coming toward us, off to one side of the road. They had countermarched.

Finally the company ahead peeled off and fell in at the tail and we followed. All the way back, men in ranks on the road yelled at the column, asking what had happened—"Did you forget to remember something?"—but by the time we came abreast (we were center brigade) theyd had enough of shouting and were quiet, standing in the road and breathing the dust we raised as we passed.

180

What had happened, Grant—after sending the
Q.M. captain with the note—had got impatient waiting for us and at two oclock, when we still hadnt
come, he sent this major to see what was the delay.
The major, surprised at not finding us on the road
nearest the river (the left arm of the V) had spurred
his horse and caught up with Wallace just in time to
prevent our marching directly into the arms of the
rebs. That was the first we knew of Grant's being
pushed back toward the Landing.

When we got to the turn-around point, within
sight of Stony Lonesome again, the sun had dropped
almost level with the treetops and we were beginning
to fag from the ten-mile hike. But there were six
miles left to travel and we went hard, marching up the
left arm of the V. Two more of Grant's staff officers
were with us by then, Colonel Birdseye McPherson
and Captain John Rawlins—I saw them when they
doubled back down the column with Wallace. They
were egging him and he was chafing under it.

The approach to Snake Creek bridge was through
a swamp. By then the sun was all the way gone and
we marched in a blue dusk. The boles of trees were
pale and the backwater glistened. It was gloomy.
Crossing the bridge we saw stragglers wading the
creek, in too big a panic to wait for us to clear the
bridge; they were in even too big a panic to wait for

181

each other, crowding past with wet feet and flopping pants legs. When we shouted down at them, calling them skulkers and cowards, they yelled back: "Youll see! Youll find out!" and such like. They said Grant was whipped and we were marching in for the surrender.

It could have been true. The firing had died for the past hour, and now it was no more than an occasional sputter. We looked at each other, wondering. But when we were across the bridge, onto the flank of the battlefield, we saw that the army was still there, what was left of it, and Buell's men were coming up from the Landing.

Then the rain began. We were put in line on the right of Sherman, along the road we had marched in on. Sherman's men had tales to tell. Most of these were descriptions of how the johnnies had overrun them, but they told some brave ones too. They said a boy in an Ohio regiment had been wounded and sent to the rear but came back a few minutes later and said to his company commander, "Captain, give me a gun. This damned fight aint got any rear."

The rain came down harder and lightning flashed. It seemed like a year since we first left Stony Lonesome.

When we had scattered that Crescent outfit, taking a batch of prisoners, we stopped to re-form and then went forward again. It was that way from then on. They wouldnt stand; they would just wait to ambush us, and every now and then they would come in a rush, screaming and yelling that wild crazy way they had. Sometimes it would shake us a bit, but generally not. They never really pushed it.

The squad worked in two sections: Sergeant Bonner with Klein and Diffenbuch, Amory, Pope and Holliday; Corporal Blake with myself and Pettigrew, Grissom and Lavery. About four oclock Diffenbuch got hit in the shoulder and we left him leaned against a tree. Diffenbuch was always a quiet one, and he didnt have much to say even then.

Raymond was coming and going but it wasnt like in training, where you could knock off when he came down. Right after Diff got hit it faired off and the sun came through. We were walking in sunlight then, dead men all over the place, some left from yesterday, twisted in ugly positions but washed clean by the rain. At one point I saw a reb and a Union man lying on opposite sides of the road, both in the standard prone position for firing. Their rifles were level and they both had one eye shut. They had the same wound, a neat red hole in the forehead, and they were stone dead, still lying there with the sights lined up—

they must have fired at the same time. Looking at them I thought of the terrible urgency they both must have felt in the last half-second before they both pulled trigger.

We were approaching the camp where Sherman's tents were standing. They had run from here yesterday morning and now we were back where it started. The rebels had formed a line along the ridge. We charged them, bayonets fixed.

That was where Pettigrew got his.

I have seen my share of men get hit (at Donelson we were caught in a tight and lost five out of twelve in less than ten minutes) but I never saw one catch it as pretty as Pettigrew did. It was quick and hard—not messy, either.

We had formed in this draw, down the slope from the hogback where the tents were pitched. The johnnies had formed in front of the tents, advanced down to what they call the military crest, and we got set to go up after them. Corporal Blake was on the right, then myself, then Pettigrew, then Lavery. Sergeant Bonner, with the other five, was over beyond Lavery.

Captain Tubbs walked up and down, checking the

platoons. Lieutenant McAfee stood fiddling with his sword. Warning came down from the right to get set. We passed it along. Then we heard Colonel Sanderson bellering and the company officers picking it up all down the line: *Charge! Charge!* and we went forward. The underbrush was thick here, creepers and briery vines twined round the trees. They made a crashing sound as we tramped through.

Toward the crest they thinned and the going was easier. That was where they opened on us. The minies came our way, singing that song they sing, and that stopped us. We hugged the ground. "All right, men!" officers called. "All right!" We crouched in the bushes waiting for the word.

Corporal Blake looked straight ahead. Pettigrew on my left was half turned in my direction, the expression on his face no different from usual. When he saw me looking at him he grinned and said something I couldnt hear because of the bullets singing and plopping into tree trunks and the rifles banging away across the draw.

While I was watching him it came: *Charge! Charge!* The whole line sprang up and started forward. I was still watching Pettigrew—I dont know why; I certainly didnt have a premonition. As he went into it, bent forward and holding his rifle across his chest, the minie struck him low in the throat (I heard it hit, above all that racket; it was like when you thump a watermelon) and he pitched forward with his arms flung out, crucified.

When I stopped and leaned over him I saw that he was almost gone already. He knew it, too. He tried to tell me something, but all that came out was three words and a bubble of blood that swelled and broke:

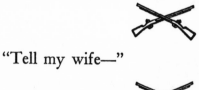

"Tell my wife—"

Grissom was wounded just as they fell back. We had taken the ridge and they were retreating across the swampy hollow, almost out of rifle range, when one of them stopped and kneeled and pinked Grissom in the thigh. He sat down with his hands over the bullet hole and began to laugh and cry at the same time, like crazy. I think he was unnerved from seeing Pettigrew get it the way he did back there in the swale. They came from the same home town, grew up together. Pettigrew saved Grissom's life once by getting the drop on a sniper at Donelson. He sat there with blood oozing between his fingers, laughing and crying, both at once, saying he'd got himself a furlough to go home to Indiana and tell Pettigrew's wife how her husband caught one quick and easy.

It turned out that was the last attack of the day. Wallace sent word to hold up. That was enough, he told us. And if anyone thinks we werent glad to hear it, let him try pushing an army of rebels through three miles of scrub oak and briers. The johnnies formed a line about a mile farther on. Probably, though, they were no more anxious to receive a charge than we were to deliver one. The way it looked to me, they were willing to call it a day if *we* were.

We sat on the grass along the ridge where Sherman's camp was. There was a creek and a bog in the draw, and all across the valley, both sides of the creek, there were dead rebs so thick you could cross it almost without touching your feet to the ground. Mostly they had been there since yesterday, and they were plenty high.

We were shifted around some then, being put in a defensive line, but there was no more fighting that day. While we were resting, the burial details went to work. The Union dead were buried by their own outfits, tagged and identified one by one and all together. But they buried the johnnies in groups near where they fell. It was interesting to watch, to see the way they did it. One of these burial trenches was near where we halted and we watched them at work.

They dug a trench about a hundred feet long, so deep that when they were finishing all we could see was flying dirt and the bright tips of their shovels. Fast as the collecting wagons brought the rebel bodies (all with their pockets turned inside-out) they laid them face-up, head-to-foot the length of the trench, each corpse resting its head between the feet of the corpse behind. It wasnt nearly as neat as it sounds, though—most of them had stiffened in awkward positions. I had noticed that many of them out on the field lay on their backs with their knees drawn up like women in labor. The diggers had to stomp the worst ones in.

The next row they laid in the other direction, still face-up but with their heads pointing the opposite way. They put them in like that, row above row, until the top ones were almost level with the grass. Then they threw in dirt—which was a relief; rebels generally rotted faster than our men. They turned blacker, too. Maybe the different rations had something to do with it. Or maybe it was just the meanness in them.

There was a big Irishman doing most of the shovel work. He seemed to enjoy it, and we got a laugh out of watching him. Throwing in dirt and smoothing it over, he would pat a dead reb on the face with the back of his shovel and say in a voice like a preacher, "Now lay there, me bye. Lay there quite till the doomsday trump. And dont ye be fomenting no more rebellions down there where ye're burrning."

Winter and Pettigrew were dead, Diffenbuch and Grissom wounded. Thirty-three and a third percent is high casualties in anybody's battle. But as usual Squad Three had caught the brunt end of the stick. Some squads hadnt lost a man. Out of one dozen hurt in Company G, four were ours, all from one squad. It just goes to show.

Bonner was a glory hunter. Anytime he could make himself look good by pushing us into a hot place, that was just what he did, and the hotter the better. Most squads liked to share the glory work, but not ours—we hogged it. Or Bonner did, which amounts to the same thing. I was talking to Klein and told him I had made up my mind to put in for a transfer.

"What ails you, Amory?" he said. "Aint you happy in your work?"

"Happy, hell," I said. "It's not fair. Thats what."

I knew it sounded foolish because I couldnt express myself very well. But I still wanted that transfer.

Watching the way they buried those rebels didnt help matters. I kept thinking maybe someday it might work out the other way round, so that the johnnies would be the ones doing the burying, and I sure didnt want to be stuffed into any ditch like that, all packed together without a marker or anything, no one to say a prayer when they let me down, no one to tell them back home how bravely I died.

When a man gives his life for his country he wants to get the worth of it, if you see what I mean.

Just before sundown they marched us away. Sherman's men moved into their camps (without even a thank-you for us winning them back) and we went over to the far right and bivouacked near Owl Creek for the night. The mess crew came down from Stony Lonesome with our supper—beans again. Night closed in while we ate. We sat in a big huddle, dirty, dog tired. The moon, in its first quarter, came up early in a cloudy sky. We bedded down.

I was so tired my legs were twitching; I couldnt even relax to go to sleep. We had paired off for warmth—Bonner and Joyner, Blake and Holliday,

Klein and Lavery, Amory and myself—all lying on
the leeward side of a blackberry clump. Amory had
organized himself a strip of blanket from one of the
cooks. It wasnt much help to me, though. Soon as he
went to sleep he began to roll, wrapping it round and
around him. For a while I tugged back, wanting my
share, but then I gave it up and just lay there. It
wasnt really cool enough for a blanket anyhow, though
it probably would be before morning. In this crazy,
no-account country a man could never tell what
weather the next hour was going to bring.

I thought about Winter and Pettigrew lying out
there dead in the woods unless one of the burial squads
got to them before nightfall. I thought for a minute:
What did those two die for? And the answer came
back: *Nothing*. It was like a voice in the night: *They
died for nothing*.

This war was so much easier for the Confederates.
I could see how they would feel different about the
whole thing, thinking they were fighting to form a
new nation the way our grandfathers did back in '76
and believing they would go down among the heroes
in the books. That was why they were so frantic in
their charges, coming against our lines with those wild
crazy yells, not minding their losses. With us it was
not that way at all. They had dared us to fight and

we fought. I thought it must be lots easier to fight *for* something than it was to fight *against* something.

But that was what the voice said. I also remembered what Corporal Blake said once. It was back in February, after Donelson; we lost six men in that fight, including one that froze to death. Blake said the rebels were really on our side. It sounded crazy but he explained it. He said they wanted the same things we wanted, the right kind of life, the right kind of government—all that—but theyd been misled by bad men. When they learned the truth they would stop fighting, he said.

As usual, though, when I began thinking stuff like that my mind got all confused, mixed up, and everything ran right back to the beginning. Winter and Pettigrew were lying dead out there in the woods and I was not. What right did I have thinking it was up to me to say why?

7 *Palmer Metcalfe Unattached*

I had lost my horse in the charge at the Fallen Timbers. Now I held onto the tailgate of a wagon filled with wounded, letting it pull me along because my boots had not been made for walking. Rain fell in slanted, steely pencilings. There was a constant murmur, the groans of the wounded as the long slow agonized column wound between weeping trees and wet brown fields; just ahead I could hear their teeth grinding and even the faint scrabbling of fingernails against the planks of the springless wagon bed. It was the same road we had followed into battle, only now we were going in the opposite direction and there was no reappearing sun to cause the troops to quicken the step.

Country people, the men in gallussed jeans, the women in gingham, stood on their porches or came out into the rain to watch us pass. They had been there Friday and Saturday, while we were going in. Now it was Tuesday and we were coming out. We half expected them to look at us reproachfully, who had passed their way so recently with such high promises, but they did not. Their faces showed nothing at all, or almost nothing. Perhaps there was sorrow but certainly there was no reproach. Truth to tell, however, my boots were hurting me to an extent that didnt encourage physiognomy.

The only face I was really conscious of was the face of a boy in the rear of the wagon; he looked out over the tailgate, our heads on a line and less than a yard apart. He wore a checkered homespun shirt which was half gone because of the way the surgeons had slit it when they took off his left arm. The skin of his face was the color of parchment, with deep azure circles under the eyes. When the jolts of the wagon were especially hard, I could hear his teeth grind and see the shape of them behind his lips. He looked at once young and old, like the boy in the tale who aged suddenly because of some unspeakable overnight experience in a haunted house. His head bobbed and weaved in time with the jogging of the wagon. He muttered to himself, saying the same thing over and over: "It dont hurt much, Captain; I just cant lift it." The stump, which was boneless, extended about four inches below his armpit. Wrapped in a rag, it swung there, a little bloody sack of bloody meat.

There were many like him in that column, men who had been wounded and lain in the woods sometimes for twenty-four hours, under the pelting rain and the shells from the gunboats, until they found strength to crawl to a collecting center or were discovered by the aid men and carried to one. From hilltops I could look forward and back and see the long column strung out for miles in both directions, twisting and squirming like a crippled snake. In almost every wagon there were men begging to be lifted out, to be laid on the ground beside the road and allowed to die in peace without the jolting. Their eyes were either hot and bright with fever or dull with shock. Whenever a wagon did halt it was only for a moment, to take out a dead one and go on again.

That was the first time I ever knew what it was to have to keep walking when everything in me said stop. About midafternoon I fell out beside the road and slit both boots at the instep with a pocket knife. That helped some, but not much. Wagons kept passing me, the mules in a slow walk, and finally I caught hold of one and let it tow me along. That way, without having to bother to do more than lift my feet and let them swing forward with the pull of the wagon,

I found my mind went idle and I saw again General Johnston the way I had seen him at two oclock Sunday afternoon, the last time I saw him alive.

One of Breckinridge's brigades had recoiled from a charge against a ridge in the Hornets Nest and the officers were having trouble getting them back into line to go forward again; they didnt want any more of it right then. General Johnston watched this for a while, then rode out front. He had taken his hat off, holding it with his left hand against his thigh, and in his right hand he held the small tin cup he had picked up in a captured camp earlier in the day. As he passed down the line he leaned sideways in the saddle and touched the points of the bayonets with the cup. It made a little clink each time.

"These must do the work," he said.

When the line had formed he rode front and center and turned his horse—Fire-eater, a thoroughbred bay —toward the crest where the Union troops were waiting.

"I will lead you!" he cried.

The men sent up a shout. General Johnston set spurs in his horse and the brigade went forward, cheering, at a run. Charging through the thickest fire I ever saw, they took the crest, halted to re-form, and stood there waving their flags and yelling so loud that the leaves on the trees seemed to tremble. The general came riding back with a smile on his face, teeth flashing beneath his mustache. His battle blood was up; his eyes had a shine like bright glass. Fire-eater was hit in four places. There were rips and tears in the general's uniform and his left bootsole had been cut nearly in half by a minie ball. He shook his foot so the dangling leather flapped. "They didnt trip me up that time!" he said, laughing.

This was the charge that began to break the Hornets Nest. I was sent with a message for Beauregard on the other flank, telling him we were moving forward again, and when I came back General Johnston's body was already stretched out for removal from the field. They told me how he died—from a wound in the right leg, a hurt so slight that anyone with a simple knowledge of tourniquets could have saved him. Doctor Yandell, his surgeon, had been with him all through the battle, but shortly before the final attack near the peach orchard, the general ordered him to establish an aid station for a group of Federal wounded he saw at one point on the field. When the doctor protested, General Johnston cut him off.

"These men were our enemies a moment ago," he said. "They are our prisoners now. Take care of them."

When I heard this, that the general had died because of his consideration for men who a short time before had been shooting at him and doing all in their power to wreck his cause, I remembered what my father had said about the South bearing within itself the seeds of defeat, the Confederacy being conceived already moribund. We were sick from an old malady, he said: incurable romanticism and misplaced chivalry, too much Walter Scott and Dumas read too seriously. We were in love with the past, he said; in love with death.

He enjoyed posing as a realist and straight thinker —war was more shovelry than chivalry, he said—but he was a highly romantic figure of a man himself and he knew it, he with his creased forehead and his tales of the war in Texas, with his empty sleeve and his midnight drinking beneath the portrait of his wife in that big empty house in New Orleans. He talked that way because of some urge for self-destruction, some compulsion to hate what he had become: an old man with a tragic life, who sent his son off to a war he was too maimed to take part in himself. It was regret. It was regret of a particular regional form.

I thought of these things while we rode beside the ambulance taking General Johnston's body back to the headquarters where we had slept the night before, where we had crawled from under our blankets at dawn to hear him say that by dark we'd water our horses in the Tennessee—which, incidentally, some

Mississippi cavalry outfit did. Beauregard had ordered the fighting stopped, intending to reorganize and complete the victory tomorrow morning. Colonel Preston and the rest of the staff, believing they could be of little use—since all that remained to be done (they thought) was to show Grant a solid front and receive his surrender—decided to accompany the body to Corinth and then by rail to St Louis Cemetery in New Orleans, where my own people had their crypts.

So I told them goodbye and watched them ride off with the ambulance in the twilight, the sound of the guns dying with a growl and a rumble back toward the river. The rain began to fall, first with a series of minute ticking sounds like a watch running down, then with a steady patter. I had come up here to fight the battle and it didnt seem proper, by my own lights, to leave before it was finished.

Soon after dark, shells from the Federal gunboats began landing in the woods. Our army was scattered all over the tableland, commands mingled past identification and strayed soldiers roaming around asking for their outfits until finally they realized they would never find them in the darkness and they might as well bed down wherever they happened to be. I slept under a tree near Beauregard's tent, not far from Shiloh Chapel; it had been Sherman's tent the night before. Every fifteen minutes (for I timed them) two of the big shells landed with a terrible crash, one after another, fragments singing through the trees. Each of them seemed near enough for me to touch it with my hand. After a while, however, like all the others on that field, I became accustomed to them. I was dog tired. I slept.

At dawn I reported to Colonel Jordan for duty with the staff. He told me to stand by. I had breakfast with him and the captured Federal general, Benjamin Prentiss. They had shared a bed in one corner of Sherman's tent the night before, and Prentiss had said: "You gentlemen have had your way today but it will be very different tomorrow. Youll see. Buell will effect a junction with Grant tonight and we'll turn the tables on you in the morning." No such thing, Colonel Jordan said, and showed him the telegram from a cavalry commander in North Alabama reporting that Buell's army was marching on Decatur. But Prentiss shook his head: "Youll see."

Dawn had come through clearly now; the sun was pushing up through the misty trees behind us. As we moved toward the breakfast table (it was done in style by Beauregard's body servant, linen tablecloth and everything) the sound of musketry broke out in a sudden clatter toward the Landing. It swelled and was sustained, the rumble of cannon joining in. We stood listening.

"There's Buell!" Prentiss cried. "Didnt I tell you so?"

He was right. The fighting was very different from that of the day before; it was clear from the first that Grant had been reinforced. Beauregard tried to do nothing more than hold him to gain time. He was hoping that Van Dorn would come with his twenty thousand troops from the Transmississippi. All morning he watched for them, hoping against hope, holding back from a general attack on a fresh force larger than his own, and looking over his shoulder from time to time.

Around noon he thought he saw them. Through the trees, across a field on the right, there was a body of men dressed in white coats and firing into an advancing line of Federals. Beauregard thought surely they were Van Dorn's men; no troops in the Army of the Mississippi wore any such outlandish get-up, while Van Dorn's westerners would be apt to wear almost anything. But when he sent me through the woods and across the field to discover who they were, I saw they were the Orleans Guard battalion, many of them friends of mine. They had come into the battle wearing their parade uniforms of dress blue, which drew the fire of their fellow Confederates. Promptly they returned it, and when a staff officer galloped up and told them they were shooting at their friends, the colonel said angrily: "I know it, Sir, but dammit we fire on everybody who fires on us!" Finally, however, they turned their coats inside-out, showing the white silk linings, and continued the battle that way.

I rode back and reported to the general. He took it well enough; at least he gave up hoping for Van Dorn. About two oclock, when the army had fallen back to a position near Sherman's camps, Colonel Jordan said to him: "General, dont you think our troops are very much in the condition of a lump of sugar thoroughly soaked in water—preserving its original shape, though ready to dissolve? Wouldnt it be judicious to get away with what we have?"

Beauregard felt the same way about it, but he was in no hurry. He sat quietly on his horse, watching the fight, his red cap pulled low on his forehead. "I intend to withdraw in a few minutes," he said calmly.

And sure enough, soon afterwards he sent couriers to the corps commanders to prepare for the withdrawal. By four oclock the action had been broken off. The three brigades of Breckinridge, or what was left of them, were posted along a stretch of high ground west of Shiloh Chapel. There was no pursuit.

I camped alone that night, on the same site we had used two nights ago when we were set to launch the attack. I was back where I started. I staked my horse in the little clearing, wrapped the blanket around me and used the saddle for a pillow. Signs of the old campfire were still there, a few charred sticks and a neat circle of ashes turned dark gray by the rain. It was quiet—as quiet as the first night I slept there. The blanket had a smell of ammonia, more pleasant than otherwise. Soon after dark there was a let-up in the rain and a few stars came through. The moon rose, faint and far and old-gold yellow, riding a bank of clouds that scurried past it, ragged as ill-sheared sheep.

Lying under that big, tattered sky and looking back over the last two days of battle, I saw that it had gone wrong for the very reason I had thought it most apt to go right. The main fault lay in the battle order I had helped to prepare, calling myself a latter-day Shakespeare because I had supplied the commas and semicolons, and ranking Colonel Jordan with Napoleon because it seemed so beautiful. Attacking the way it directed—three corps in line from creek to creek, one behind another, with the successive lines feeding reinforcements piecemeal into the line ahead—divisions and regiments and even companies had become so intermingled that commanding officers lost touch with their men and found themselves leading strangers who never before had heard the sound of their voices. Coördination was lost all down the line. By midafternoon of the first day it was no longer an army of corps and divisions; it was a mass of men crowded into an approximate battle formation. The one strong, concerted push—left and center and right together—which would have ended the battle Sunday evening, forcing the Federal army into the Tennessee, could not be made because coördination had been lost. At that stage it was no longer even a battle: it was a hundred furious little skirmishes, strung out in a crooked line.

> *We but teach*
> *Bloody instructions, which being taught, return*
> *To plague th'inventor.*

There you go, I told myself, reincarnating Shakespeare again.

I slid into unconsciousness so smoothly I couldnt tell where the spilt-milk thinking left off and the dreaming began. The pleasant pungent odor of ammonia was all around me. The last thing I remember, unless indeed it was something in the dream, was the sound of my horse cropping grass. Next thing I knew, Tuesday was dawning.

Breckinridge held his troops in position; the rest of the army took the road for Corinth. I stayed behind, unattached till I joined a body of about two hundred Tennessee cavalry under Colonel N. B. Forrest, a tall, swarthy man with a black chin-beard and a positive manner. He was much admired for having brought

his regiment out of Donelson instead of surrendering,
but I knew men who, believing that an officer in our
army should be a gentleman as well as a soldier, would
have refused to serve under him because he had been
a slave dealer in Memphis before the war. They also
objected to a habit he had of using the flat of his saber
and even his fists on his men when he became aroused.
I was surprised to find him soft-spoken.

When the other corps had gotten a start, Breckinridge commenced his withdrawal, leaving the cavalry
to discourage pursuit. As a matter of fact there was
no pursuit for us to discourage, yet. We stayed there
an hour, Forrest's regiment and a few scattered
troopers from Mississippi and Kentucky and Texas.
Then we drew off, following in the rear of Breckinridge. So far we hadnt seen a single Federal. Perhaps
it could be called a retreat—doubtless Grant would
call it that—but it was a retreat without pressure. We
fell back when we got good and ready.

Two hours south of the battlefield, on the road to
Monterey, we crossed a wide swampy hollow rising
to a crest at the far side with a notch where the road
went through. A branch of Lick Creek flowed through
this boggy swale and trees had been felled on both
sides of the stream, doubtless a logging project begun
by some of the natives, then abandoned when the war
began; they had finished the cutting but hadnt got

started on the clearing and hauling. It was known as the Fallen Timbers, a mean-looking stretch of ground nearly a mile across, with jagged stumps and felled trees crisscrossed and interlaced with vines and knee-high weeds. I thought to myself what a mean, ugly place it would be to fight in.

Forrest, however, had been watching for just such a position ever since we began the march. From time to time he would rein in his horse and look at the terrain, seeking a place to make a stand in case of attack. We couldnt believe that Grant, reinforced by fresh troops equal in numbers to his retiring enemy, would let us get away without some sort of pursuit, or at least the show of one, if for no other reason than to be able to report that he had chased us. The crest beyond the swale afforded an excellent defensive position. I could see that Forrest had already decided to form a line there (his eyes lit up the minute it came into sight) even before one of his scouts with the rear point, a man they called Polly—I wondered if that was really his name—rode up and reported a heavy column of cavalry and infantry coming hard down the road behind us.

Forrest gave his horse its head, riding fast for the notch where the road rose out of the slough to pass over the crest, and we followed. There were between three and four hundred of us, half his own Tennessee

troops, the rest gathered from three commands assigned to him for rear-guard duty. In one group there
were Texas rangers. They had lost their colonel in
yesterday's fight and now were under Major Tom
Harrison, lanky men wearing high-heeled boots, the
rowels of their spurs as big and bright as silver dollars.
Colonel Wirt Adams had half a hundred Mississippians, wild-looking in checkered shirts and a crazy
assortment of wide-brimmed hats. They appeared to
have been engaged in a six-month contest to see who
could grow the fiercest beard. Captain John Morgan
led a handful of Kentuckians. They were soberly
dressed and riding superior horses. The captain himself was tall and fair-faced. With his delicate hands
and waxed mustache, he looked as neat and cool as if
he had seen no fighting. We went through the notch
at a canter, and Forrest soon had us spread out in a
position along the crest.

Then we saw the Federals, a brigade of them with
a regiment of cavalry attached, strung out in approach-
march formation on the road beyond the Fallen
Timbers. They must have seen us almost as soon as
we saw them, for the point signaled danger and the
whole blue mass pulled up in a halt on the slope giving
down to the creek. There was a delay while an officer
on a big gray horse rode forward—a ranker, for he

had his staff in tow—and sat there studying us with his field glasses.

It didnt take long. He soon put the glasses back in their case, gave some instructions, and the brigade began to deploy for action. One regiment was thrown forward as a skirmish line, the cavalry backing them up and guarding their flanks. The remainder of the brigade was massed in attack-formation two or three hundred yards in the rear. The blare of the bugle reached us faintly from across the swale. They came on, looking good according to the manual.

That was when Forrest gave me my first lesson in his kind of tactics, and it had nothing to do with the manual. I had heard something about his unorthodox methods of fighting; I had even been told that boldness was the basis of his success—he fought "by ear," they said. But nothing I'd heard had led me to expect him to accept battle with a whole brigade of Yank infantry, when all he had to oppose them was three hundred and fifty unorganized cavalrymen, most of them frazzled from seven days on the go, including two days of steady fighting.

I thought to myself, Surely he's not going to have us *stay* here. Surely he doesnt expect us to hold them.

They appeared small, automaton-like, as they picked their way over and around the fallen trees, lifting their knees to keep their feet from getting tangled in the vines. By the time they were halfway across, some on this side of the stream, some yet on the other, their line had lost all semblance of order —they could hardly have been more disorganized if we had opened on them with artillery. I looked over toward the notch and saw Forrest giving orders to his bugler. The sound of the horn rang out. Just as I was thinking, 'Surely he cant expect us to hold this ridge against a whole brigade,' the bugle was blaring the charge and Forrest put spurs to his horse; he was leading the way. He was obeying his instinct for never standing to receive an attack when he had a chance to deliver one.

One minute I was expecting to be told to retire, and the next the bugle was blaring the charge. For a moment I mistrusted my ears. It caught me so unprepared I was still sitting there with my mouth dropped open, reins lax in my hands, when the line of horsemen surged forward, galloping down the slope. I finally caught up, the hoofs drumming like thunder, the horses breathing hoarse, the men all yelling. The Texans had dropped the reins onto their horses' necks and were going into the charge with both hands free, one for the saber, the other for the revolver. The checkered-shirt Mississippians carried shotguns across their thighs, whiskers blowing wild in the wind.

Forrest was fifty yards out front, standing in the stirrups and swinging a saber.

Most of the skirmishers had begun to run before we hit them, scrambling among the fallen trees and tripping over the vines. Those who stood were knocked sprawling by a blast from revolvers and shotguns fired at twenty paces. I caught a glimpse of Forrest hacking and slashing, riding them down. His saber looked ten feet long; it flashed and glinted. All around me horses were tripping and falling, crashing and thrashing in the underbrush, snorting and whinnying with terror. We had scattered the skirmishers, but Forrest didnt stop. He rode on, still standing and brandishing the saber, charging the Federal cavalry behind the skirmishers. They were in complete disorder even before we struck them, some wheeling their mounts toward the rear, others pressing toward the front, all panicky, firing their carbines in the air. It was the wildest craziest melee a man could imagine, one of those things you would have to see to believe. But it was true, all right, and I was in the very middle of it.

That was when my horse went down, struck in the knee of the off foreleg by a wild shot—Union or Confederate, Lord knows which—and before I even had time to think what was happening, the whole front end of him broke down and I went sailing over his head. I landed on my chest, spread-eagle; my wind went out with a rush. I got on my hands and knees, trying to breathe and trying to breathe, but no breath would come. My breathing apparatus had been knocked out of action. I was hoping for someone to give me a whack on the back (Rebel or Yank or even one of the horses: I didnt care) when I looked up and saw something that made me forget that breathing had anything to do with living.

Forrest was still out front and he was still charging. He had broken the skirmish line, scattered the cavalry, and now he was going after the main body, the remainder of the brigade, which stood in solid ranks to receive the charge. The trouble was, he was charging by himself. Everyone else had reined in when the cavalry scattered; they saw the steady brigade front and turned back to gather prisoners. But not Forrest. He was fifty yards beyond the farthest horseman, still waving that saber and crying "Charge! Charge!" when he struck the blue infantry line, breaking into it and plunging through the ranks. They closed the gap behind him. He was one gray uniform, high on his horse above a sea of blue. I could hear the soldiers shouting, "Kill him!" "*Kill* the goddam rebel!" "Knock him off his horse!"

Then Forrest saw what had happened and began to haul on the reins, trying to turn back toward his own men. But as the horse wheeled, lashing out with its hoofs while Forrest slashed with his saber, I saw one of the soldiers—a big heavy-set corporal—shove the muzzle of his rifle into the colonel's hip and pull the trigger. The force of the ball lifted Forrest sideways and clear of the saddle, but he regained his seat and held onto the reins, the horse still kicking and plunging and Forrest still hacking and slashing.

He was facing our lines by then, clearing a path with his saber, and as he came out of the mass of blue uniforms and furious white faces, he reached down and grabbed one of the soldiers by the nape of the neck, swung him onto the crupper of his horse, and galloped back to our lines, using the Federal as a shield against the bullets fired after him. When he was out of range he flung the soldier off, the man's head striking one of the jagged stumps with a loud crack, and rode up to where we were waiting. I discovered that my breath had come back—I was breathing short and shallow from excitement.

That was the end of the fighting. The ball that wounded Forrest was the last that drew blood in the battle of Shiloh. The repulse at the Fallen Timbers put an end to whatever desire the Union army may have had for pursuit. From the crest where we had begun our charge we watched them collect their dead and wounded and turn back the way they had come. That was the last we saw of them.

Out of the group of prisoners taken here, I heard one tell a questioner that he was from Sherman's division and that the officer we had watched while he studied the field with his glasses was Sherman himself. I was afoot then, and one of the Tennessee troopers let me ride behind him. We caught up with the column on the Corinth road and doubled it a ways until the horse began to fag and I got down. It was shank's mare for me from there on in.

Having seen Sherman face to face that way—even if I had not recognized him at the time—I kept remembering the crazy notion I had had, while going to sleep the night before the battle, about capturing him and making him admit he was wrong about what he'd said that Christmas Eve a year and three months ago, at the Louisiana State Military Academy; he was superintendent.

That year I had the measles and couldnt go home for the holidays. It was gloomy in the big infirmary with all the other cadets away enjoying turkey and fireworks, so as soon as I got better—though I still wasnt allowed to get up and had to keep the shades drawn—Sherman had me moved into the spare bedroom in his quarters. The place had a strong odor of niter paper, which he burned for his asthma. I would come awake in the night hearing him cough. He was about twenty pounds underweight and we all thought he was in consumption.

That Christmas Eve he had supper in his sitting room with Professor Boyd, a Virginian who taught Latin and Greek. The door was ajar and I could see them sitting in front of the fire, enjoying their after-supper cigars. Presently a servant came in with a newspaper which had arrived from town. Sherman had his back to me, less than a dozen feet away, and when he spread the paper I saw the headline big and black: South Carolina had seceded, voted herself out of the Union.

He read it rapidly. Then he tossed the paper into Mr Boyd's lap and walked up and down the room while the professor read it. Finally he stopped pacing and stood in front of Mr Boyd, shaking a bony finger in his face, addressing him as if he had the whole South in the room. "You people of the South dont know what you are doing," he said. "This country will be drenched in blood, and God only knows how it will end. It is all folly, madness, a crime against civilization."

He resumed his pacing, still talking. "You people speak so lightly of war. You dont know what youre talking about. War is a terrible thing!" He reached the end of the room and came back, still talking. "You mis-

216

take, too, the people of the North. They are a peaceable people but an earnest people, and they will fight too—they are not going to let this country be destroyed without a mighty effort to save it. Besides, where are your men and appliances of war to contend against them? The North can make a steam engine, locomotive or railway car; hardly a yard of cloth or a pair of shoes can you make. You are rushing into war with one of the most powerful, ingeniously mechanical and determined people on earth —right at your doors." He stopped and frowned.

"You are bound to fail. Only in your spirit and determination are you prepared for war. In all else you are totally unprepared, with a bad cause to start with. At first you will make headway, but as your limited resources begin to fail—shut out from the markets of Europe as you will be—your cause will begin to wane. If your people will but stop and think, they must see that in the end youll surely fail."

He made another turn at the end of the room, his hands clasped beneath his coattail. As he came back I saw the firelight glisten on the tears in his beard; they sparkled like jewels hung in the russet whiskers.

The memory of Sherman pacing the floor, saying we were bound to fail, stayed with me constantly through the first year of the war. It rose in my mind while I was joining up, during the heart-breaking attempt to hold the shaky line that snapped at Bowling Green and Donelson, during the long retreat from Kentucky into Mississippi, and during the march to battle between those two creeks on the tableland above Pittsburg Landing. He was the first American I ever heard refer to the cause of constitutional liberty as a bad one: I knew he was wrong there, I could discount that. But some of the other things—the threat of blockade, for instance, the comparison of our mechanical powers and resources—were not so easily set aside.

It was not until the charge at the Fallen Timbers that I found the answer, the oversight in his argument. He hadnt mentioned Forrest or men like Forrest, men who did not fight as if odds made the winner, who did not necessarily believe that God was on the side of the big battalions, who would charge a brigade with half a regiment of weary men and send that brigade stumbling back to its tents demoralized and glad to be let alone. The army that had Forrest—and would *use* him—could afford to put its trust in something beside mechanical aptitude or numbers.

This was the answer to all he had said, and it made my future certain. I said goodbye to staff work, the placing of words on paper where they looked good and played you false, and determined that when I got back to Corinth I would get myself another horse and enlist under Forrest, commissioned or not. Or if it turned out that Forrest did not recover from the wound he had received that day (which seemed likely) I would enlist under someone as much like him as possible—Wirt Adams, say, or John Morgan. I was through with visions of facing Sherman in his tent and forcing him at pistol point to admit that he was wrong. The time to face him down would be after the war, when no pistol would be needed and the fact could speak for itself.

It was a load lifted from my brain—I was like a man long troubled by a bad dream who suddenly discovers he can sleep without its return. Instead of being a prophecy, as I had feared, the things Sherman said that Christmas Eve were a goad, a gauntlet thrown down for me to pick up. I hoped he would last the war so I could tell him.

These things were in my mind as I traveled south on the Corinth road, first on horseback behind the Tennessee trooper, then trudging along in boots that got tighter and tighter across the instep. They had been made for me by Jeanpris Brothers in New Orleans and they were strictly for riding. When I had slit them and rejoined the column they felt fine at first, but soon the rain began. I started to fag. The boots got worse than ever; it was like walking on pinpoints. Holding onto the tailgate of the wagon was a help. My feet did not touch the ground as long that way, it seemed, and they no longer had to propel my body forward. All they had to do was swing one-two one-two with the pull of the mules, the rhythm of it washing all else out of my mind until I began to remember General Johnston and the way he died at high tide of the battle.

"It dont hurt much, Captain," the boy said. "I just cant lift it."

Then it was late afternoon, the rain coming slow and steady, not really unpleasant once you were all the way wet, provided you were tired enough not to complain —which I was—or had something else hurting you enough to keep your mind off the rain—which I had. Both sides of the road were littered with equipment thrown away by soldiers and by teamsters to lighten their loads: extra caissons and fifth wheels abandoned by the artillerymen when their horses got too weak to haul them, bowie knives and Bibles and playing cards which some of the men had managed to hold onto all the way to the fight and through the fighting, and occasional stragglers sitting beside the road with their heads on their knees, taking a breather.

As twilight drew in, the wind veered until it came directly out of the north, whistling along the boughs of roadside trees. Thunder rumbled and the rain was like icy spray driven in scuds along the ground. It grew dark suddenly, not with the darkness of night but with the gathering of clouds, a weird, eerie refulgence. Thunder pealed and long zigzags of lightning forked down, bright yellow against the sky. The air had a smell of electricity; when I breathed it came against my tongue with a taste like brass. The rain turned to sleet, first powdery, almost as soft as snow, then larger and larger until it was hail, the individual stones as large as partridge eggs, plopping against the mud and rattling against the wagon bed with a clattering sound like a stick being raked along a picket fence. Within an hour it was two inches deep everywhere, in the fields, on the roofs of cabins, and in the wagons where the wounded lay.

We crossed the state line, entering Mississippi again. The storm had passed by then, the worst of it, and what was left of daylight filtered through. The countryside was strange and new, all white and clean except for the muddy puddles. On a rail fence beside the road a brown thrasher sat watching the column go past, and for some reason he singled me out, the steady yellow bead of his eye following me, the long bill turning slowly in profile until I came abreast: whereupon he sprang away from the rail with a single quick motion, his wings and narrow tail the color of dusty cinnamon, and was gone.

In the wagon the wounded were mostly too sore to brush the sleet and hail away, or perhaps they had reached a stage where they didnt care. They lay with it piled between their legs and in their laps. It filled the wrinkles in their uniforms so that the angry red of their wounds stood out sharp against its whiteness. Up front, sitting with his back to the driver, there was a man whose face I avoided. His jaw had been shot away but his tongue was still there; it hung down on his throat like a four-in-hand tie.

The boy who had lost an arm was better now, as if the gusts of rain and sleet and hail had cleared his mind. Above the circles of pain and fatigue, his eyes were bright. He had begun to look around, first at the ones in the wagon with him, then at the others walking alongside. Facing me over the tailgate he suddenly seemed to realize where he was, that the column was heading for Corinth. He wet his lips and looked at me. For the first time, except for the raving, he spoke. "Lieutenant . . ." His voice was weak; he tried again. "Lieutenant . . ."

"Yes?"

"Lieutenant—did we get whupped?"

I said I supposed they would call it that. He sort of shrank back into himself, as if this was what he had expected, and did not speak again. It was night now and the stars were out, though the moon had not risen. My boots made a crunching sound in the sleet. Soon the lamps of Corinth came into sight, and along the roadside there were women with hot coffee.

Note

Historical characters in this book speak the words they spoke and do the things they did at Shiloh. Many of the minor incidents also occurred, even when here they are assigned to fictional persons; I hope the weather is accurate too. This was made possible by the records left by men who were there — in the memoirs of Grant and Sherman, in the series of articles collected under the title *Battles and Leaders of the Civil War*, and particularly in the reports of officers, forwarded through channels and collected in Volume X of *The War of the Rebellion: a Compilation of the Official Records of the Union and Confederate Armies*. There you hear the live men speak.

General Johnston's biography, written by his son William Preston Johnston and published by Appleton in 1878, remains the consummate study of Shiloh. It was this book which first drew my interest and it was this book to which I returned most often for information.

Section Five is based in part on a paper, "Forrest at Shiloh," read by Major G. V. Rambaut before the Confederate Historical Society of Memphis and published in the 19 January 1896 *Commercial Appeal.* Robert Selph Henry's biography of Forrest, published by Bobbs-Merrill in 1944, contributed much to this section as well as to others.

The two best modern studies of the battle are found in Lloyd Lewis' *Sherman: Fighting Prophet* (Harcourt, Brace, 1932) and Stanley F. Horn's *The Army of Tennessee* (Bobbs-Merrill, 1941) — I have drawn on both.

Authorities at Shiloh National Military Park gave me the run of the battlefield, surely one of the best preserved in the world, and were invaluable in locating the scenes of action. Also I think no one who studies our Civil War should make a list of acknowledgments without mentioning the photographs of Mathew Brady and the writings of Douglas Southall Freeman.

—S. F.

ABOUT THE AUTHOR

Although he now makes his home in Memphis, Tennessee, SHELBY FOOTE comes from a long line of Mississippians. He was born in Greenville, Mississippi, and attended school there until he entered the University of North Carolina. During World War II he served in the European theater as a captain of field artillery. In addition to *Shiloh*, he has written four other novels—*Tournament, Follow Me Down, Love in a Dry Season* and *Jordan County*—and is now at work on a sixth, *September September*. He was awarded three Guggenheim fellowships in the twenty-year course of writing his monumental three-volume history *The Civil War: A Narrative—I. Fort Sumter to Perryville; II. Fredericksburg to Meridian; III. Red River to Appomattox*.